The remo...
expressi...

"I've changed my mind about you, Valentine. You're staying on the estate."

Valentine was immobile. "Why?"

"Have you forgotten my telling you what I'd like to do to the woman who destroyed Philip?" he inquired silkily. "I said I'd take her and break her, Valentine."

She shuddered inwardly. "And I will," he went on. "I'll see you at my feet before I let you go, sweetheart. You told me earlier—and with what pride—that you never wept for my cousin. Well, *I'll* make you weep—to rival the Cape winter rains."

"In that case I'm giving notice," she said coldly.

"You'll stay," he said.

"Vengeance doesn't become you, Kemp."

"Only civilized women merit civilized treatment," he said with such appalling hatred that she cringed at the thought of what was going to follow.

Harlequin Presents
by Jayne Bauling

247—WALK IN THE SHADOWS
505—WAIT FOR THE STORM
663—VALENTINE'S DAY

These books may be available at your local bookseller.

For a free catalog listing all titles currently available,
send your name and address to:

Harlequin Reader Service
P.O. Box 52040, Phoenix, AZ 85072-9988
Canadian address: Stratford, Ontario N5A 6W2

JAYNE BAULING

valentine's day

Harlequin Books

TORONTO • NEW YORK • LONDON
AMSTERDAM • PARIS • SYDNEY • HAMBURG
STOCKHOLM • ATHENS • TOKYO • MILAN

Harlequin Presents first edition February 1984
ISBN 0-373-10663-7

Original hardcover edition published in 1982
by Mills & Boon Limited

CHAPTER ONE

'I'M a woman with a past,' she said mysteriously, silvered eyelids fringed with long dark lashes sweeping briefly down over sapphire eyes.

'I'll bet,' one of the young men said, and the other two laughed sycophantically.

Her red lips curved slightly in satisfaction, for it had been her intention to amuse rather than intrigue, since she had spoken with more truth than they must ever know. There was pain enough in her own constant awareness of that truth; to have them know it would only add to its weight. They looked at her admiringly now, neither lasciviously as older men did, nor worshipfully as other men, also young but less sure of themselves, had been known to do; as Philip had done a year ago, and Henry van Wyk had done tonight, she recalled regretfully.

Their eyes still rested on her as she raised her glass to her lips and sipped carefully at the local sparkling wine made by the méthode champénoise, for she was as romantic-looking as her name, which was Valentine, and they were young, male and unmarried. They were also, probably, unimaginative and superficial, thus suiting her peculiar requirements, and there were others present who recognised these characteristics and despised her choice of company. But why not entertain them? Blessed at birth with the twin gifts of mental and physical allure, she still suffered like a lost soul, for they brought misjudgment. But to subdue either would be to deny truth, she thought with weary defiance.

Allowing her attention to wander, Valentine turned her dark head slightly, seeking again the tall man who had looked at her with such scorn a few minutes previously. She had felt then that familiar regret for the lack of understanding that came from those who only saw her act. Yet what else could she expect when all her behaviour was a pretence designed to cloak truth?

Up on the large verandah of the house couples were dancing to the sophisticated rhythm of the hired band; people strolled about the lawns in their finery; and others were, like herself and her three companions, remaining at the prettily appointed tables under the trees in which hung gold and silver lights. Beyond the garden were the vineyards, and beyond those a backdrop of mountains like cardboard cut-outs which had been draped with black velvet. Even with the lights in the trees killing the frailer light of stars, it was a beautiful setting for a party, and Valentine was consciously enjoying herself. Born and brought up in the Cape, she had always been attracted by the wine-producing Boland region of the province where the old estates had names, French, Dutch, German and even some English, which evoked images of beauty. Like Fleurmont ... She had even, years ago, contemplated taking her degree at Stellenbosch before logic had caused her to realise that she would be better off at the University of Cape Town where lectures were given in her home language. Thus her coming to this region had been delayed, and in the end it had been tragedy which had driven her here. Philip's tragedy.

Carefully concealing the sudden sad nature of her thoughts with a smile, she gave her attention back to her three companions for a few seconds before once more looking for the man. He was not where she had first seen him, but a moment later she located him, still standing alone, completely relaxed and at ease, surveying the scene about him with a certain detached interest which suggested that he was a late arrival.

Valentine wanted him to look at her again, willed him to do so, and after a few seconds he did, leaving her wondering with a breathless sense of shock if mere coincidence had caused him to turn his head or if he had been sensitive to the exertions of her mind.

He was tall, very tall, and well built under his casual clothes, without any surplus flesh, and she realised that he was probably missing some of his usual weight; he had the look of a man who had been driving himself too hard for too long.

Bracing herself, she once more let her sparkling sapphire eyes move up to his face, knowing too well what she would see there. His lips curled derisively; he had a sensual yet somehow ironic mouth, and Valentine knew instinctively that a lot of living lay behind that expression. His jawline hinted at a forceful character, as did the strong line of his nose and, like her, he had high cheekbones.

His mockery of a smile frustrated her, even hurt her, but she had learnt to bury hurt under defiance by now, rebelling against the inevitability of pain, so she returned it with a cool one of her own, challenging him. He was probably in the latter half of his thirties, a man of uncompromising character and, too, a beautiful man. Valentine thought wistfully—I could match him, yet not bring him to his knees. Never that.

She had surprised herself, and hastened to mask the fact. Match him. She looked again and, beyond the scorn of his expression, recognised a strength that also lay in herself, an intrinsic resilience.

Excitement quivered like a taut wire within her. Was this the end of the road she had travelled, so often in despair during the last year? She was being too impressed, she endeavoured to persuade herself, caught off balance by an attractive physique, sensual, intelligent features and clean, thick, light brown, almost fair hair. He was probably married anyway. At his age. And if he knew the truth about her——

Certainly he didn't appear to share her sense of recognition. He had started to look bored, idly glancing at her companions, then casting her a final ironic look before turning to greet Gary's father, their host. She watched him still, watched the strange blend of grace and restlessness in his movements, and wondered about him.

'Valli?'

An old unhappiness stirred and a faint crease disturbed the serenity of her forehead as the shortening of her name recalled a time she was striving to forget.

'Valentine,' she corrected clearly, but forced an unconcerned smile lest they wonder too much at her insistence.

For a moment she couldn't remember which name went with which face, for they were so similar in many ways, these three. Desmond was the redhead, of course, a little older, but a little less sure of himself, not being heir to a wine estate as the other two were. Gary was the flaxen Saxon, as she had mentally dubbed him, and Adam was Adam Ducaine, son of the estate next to Fleurmont on which she was employed. Emma Ducaine was his sister.

'I'm going to check up on you,' Emma had said. 'I owe it to Fleurmont. That lawyer must have been out of his mind, employing just anyone!'

But nothing seemed to have resulted from the threat, since her parents and brother had continued to treat her with their initial friendliness and hospitality, Valentine reflected with some relief.

That had been six months ago, when she had taken up her job at Fleurmont in the absence of the new owner. She had been desperate to get out of Cape Town at the time, imagining recognition and censure at every turn, and the job had seemed ideal. The lawyer handling the various affairs of the estate hadn't explained any more than it was her business to know: that the owner and his wife had been killed in a road accident and their heir, a nephew, would not be able to take up residence for some months owing to contractual obligations. The job she was to do had been shared by the wives of the owner and cellarmaster. Now Mrs Hattingh felt unable to continue with it on her own as she had a five-year-old daughter to look after.

Valentine had gratefully accepted the opportunity to

escape and had come to the Boland to find friends in James and Sylvie Hattingh and among the families on neighbouring estates, for though an élite community, it was a friendly one, with each vintner desiring the well-being of all estates rather than just his own. They didn't question her too much, but they had wanted her to be happy, for Fleurmont's sake, and this was far from being the first such party she had been invited to. She now lived amid luxurious surroundings and had been introduced to a style of living she appreciated, and if memory kept her wary, she thought that was all to the good. She was marking time, it was true, but she was working, which was the important thing. Unlike Philip, she believed that any disaster, any destruction of dreams, had to be worked through. However painful, and it was, that was the only way to survive, and her intense pride would not allow her to be anything other than a survivor.

Occasionally she wondered nervously if any of her new acquaintances recognised her face or connected Valentine with Valli, the name she had preferred up until a year ago. If they did, their manners were too good to allow them to comment; perhaps, she often thought hopefully, they were even too refined to read that particular type of Sunday newspaper. Either way, dozens of other scandals had succeeded that which had given her her brief agonising experience of notoriety, and people's memories were mercifully short.

All in all, she was wont to reflect, this business of surviving, ducking and dodging the blows that could destroy her, was working out fairly well. It wearied her, but it worked. Additionally, she had a well paid job which she enjoyed. The only potential shadow in the future, as opposed to the many lying over the past, was the impending arrival of her official boss. There had been some resentful muttering among both neighbouring vintners and Fleurmont's labourers about the way he was taking his time over coming to take up his inheritance, but Valentine knew Kemp Irvine's reputation as one of South Africa's foremost media men, the maker of superb documentaries, some of which were made under conditions of extreme adversity, and the Fleurmont estate's lawyer had confirmed that the new owner was unable to return to the Cape for some time.

'Not that he's any stranger to Fleurmont and the cycle of wine-making,' Sylvie Hattingh had told Valentine. 'James and I weren't here in those days, of course, but I believe his parents' marriage broke up quite early and he consequently spent a lot of time with his uncle and aunt. I wonder when he'll arrive?'

They had all said that, so many times, but finally a telegram had come, stating briefly that he would be arriving shortly, and Valentine was looking forward to meeting the man whose work she had admired. He would be here just in time for the start of harvesting which took place from mid-February to late March, and when that was over, perhaps Fleurmont would have its own party.

'Shall we dance again?' Gary asked a little later when Valentine had danced with each of them in turn and then returned to their table with him while Adam and Desmond danced with daughters of neighbouring estates.

'I don't think so, thank you, Gary,' she declined with her most charming smile. 'In fact, in a little while I'm going to go home. Did I tell you that my boss is due to arrive any day how? I want to be at my best when he does, and I won't be if I turn this into a late night.'

'You're always at your best, angel,' Gary said gallantly, and meant it.

Valentine gave him a sideways look which acknowledged the compliment then stood up swiftly.

'But before I leave, there's someone I have to speak to,' she murmured, and drifted away.

He had observed her while she was dancing, the man who had attracted her attention earlier, and she was determined to know who he was. She was not unduly shy, but for a year now a self-protective act had given the illusion of even more confidence than she actually possessed, but still the thought of approaching him was alien to her instinctive creed of behaviour. Additionally, his various glances had signalled no sort of approval, but Valentine was now governed by something more powerful than the rationalising of her mind, and it slightly subdued her nervousness. At least she was at her best tonight, mind and senses alert.

Her dress, she knew, was a dream; a confection, as she liked to call it, and she was tall enough and slender enough to carry it off with panache. Until she had seen it, she had not thought that white could be as flamboyant as strong colours. Made of alternate panels of snowy tulle and lace through which her gleaming skin could faintly be discerned, it had a fullish skirt below a tightly swathed bodice and one shoulder was bare, while over the upper part of her left arm cascaded a lacy flounce of a sleeve. With it, she wore high silver sandals and fine silver jewellery, and there was silver glitter in her shiny dark hair.

Moving with characteristic grace, she wandered, seemingly inadvertently, into the orbit of the tall man, and knew that he must have seen her. Her pulses fluttered as tense expectation assailed her. Why was she behaving like this?

Henry van Wyk appeared, giving her a shy appealing look, all his adulation visible in his dark eyes, and Valentine produced a small, coolly discouraging smile. She saw him flush and hated the necessity of inflicting pain but, well schooled by now, she knew it was better now, because still superficial. To encourage first would create a greater hurt later on.

She looked for the man, found him looking back at her, and felt suddenly frightened.

'Poor Henry,' he drawled.

'He's only a boy,' Valentine replied quietly. She couldn't be other than she was, but there would never be another Philip, she had sworn from the depths of her agony.

'Therefore no good to you?' he taunted, but it was the

most attractive voice she had heard, the enunciation perfect and every word beautifully articulated. 'The archetypal bitch-goddess, no less. You look as if you'd bend and break, but there's steel beneath the pretty packaging, isn't there?'

'I hope so.' It was a disquieting exchange, but to discard her act would be to appear vulnerable. 'You may understand one day.'

His eyes were a bright, intense blue and very hard as he looked back at her. They were surrounded by tiny fine lines drawn there, she thought, by both pain and laughter. His gaze dropped, quite deliberately and with a certain insolence, to her firm breasts and slender waist, and Valentine felt a churning excitement within her.

Then he looked at her face again, and, smiling sardonically, shook his head slightly.

'Oh no, sweetheart, not one day, although I think I understand already,' he said coolly, rejecting her. 'You're quite amazingly lovely, as you evidently know, both stylish and sexy, but most men in their right senses would run a mile when they saw you coming.'

'But you're not most men, are you?' she prompted daringly, slanting a bewitching smile up at him, for though she was tall, he was still taller. But already the effort was draining her.

'Agreed, but I am in my right senses.' He paused and his smile took on an element of cruelty. 'You're behaving very badly, you know, making a fool of yourself. Did your mother never tell you that however much the order of things may have changed, men still prefer and always will prefer to be the hunters?'

It wasn't working, she thought sadly. Even he was only really seeing the outward Valentine, and how could she reveal the inner vulnerability? To do so would give him the power to strike her down.

'I saw you watching me earlier,' she suggested mildly in her low, clear voice.

'Ah, yes!' He laughed suddenly. 'I was wondering who

she could be, as decorative as a meringue!'

'Yes!' Valentine shared his laughter, smoothing the skirt of her dress with long slender fingers tipped with crimson. She was grateful for the diversion—it gave her time. 'Confection was the word I had thought of . . . But meringues are all air and sweetness, you know.'

'And there's more to you than that, I'm beginning to learn,' he responded. 'What's your name?'

She hesitated momentarily, but perhaps he didn't notice. 'Valentine.'

'Your first name?'

'Valentine,' she repeated.

'God! It would have to be something like that,' he derided amusedly. 'As outrageous as the women it adorns. And women . . . ladies of your kind don't have surnames.'

'Are you married?' she digressed as sudden fear touched her over-excited mind, making her forget to dissemble.

'You'd ask that before asking my name?' He raised mocking eyebrows. 'Would it deter you if I was?'

She shuddered delicately, but it was her lips, suddenly sad in shape, that revealed how genuine she was. 'Definitely.'

'I can't claim the protection of a wife, I'm afraid. Nevertheless, I'm sufficiently armoured against women like you, so you can take your witchcraft elsewhere, Valentine no-surname, and weave your spells about some other unwary male,' he informed her coldly. 'Young Henry van Wyk would appear to be a willing victim . . . He's quite as eligible as Adam and Gary whom you were entertaining earlier, or didn't you know that?'

Already he was looking beyond her, with a slight smile, towards someone who was approaching them, she realised frustratedly.

I know you, I've looked for you, she thought with wild anguish—so why didn't he recognise her in return? All the rigidly repressed passion of her nature, merely hinted at in her sensual lower lip, was calling to him, and he was ignoring the call. Could she be mistaken?

Mr and Mrs Ducaine and their daughter Emma reached them at that moment.

'Kemp!'

They were smiling in warm welcome and only Emma's smile faltered when they turned to Valentine, although her mother's grew a little frosty.

'When did you arrive, Kemp?' Emma questioned eagerly.

'How are you all? I arrived in Johannesburg this afternoon, flew down to Cape Town this evening, picked up a new car and drove out immediately,' he informed them, arching an enquiring eyebrow when he saw the mischievous delight transforming Valentine's lovely face, but she held her peace. Enlightenment would come.

'About time too,' Mr Ducaine, stocky and greying, commended cheerfully. 'And Valentine—are you pleased with your new boss?'

'I've only just this minute realised that he is my boss, Mr Ducaine,' she told him. 'Valentine McLaren, Mr Irvine.'

'My God!' He looked at her, eyes brilliant with contemptuous amusement. 'I was imagining one of your bright sensible P.R. types when that lawyer told me he'd hired someone—but I suppose the man is as fallible as anyone.'

'Anyone, except you?' Valentine murmured, recalling his remark about being armoured against women like her.

'Clever as well as beautiful,' he commented.

Emma was looking disconsolate and now she broke in abruptly, 'The two of you were talking together long enough, Kemp. How was it that you never got round to introducing yourselves?'

'Oh, names aren't of much importance in the sort of situation in which we found ourselves, Emma,' he said lightly, flicking a cruel glance at Valentine. 'You see, Valentine was trying to pick me up.'

Valentine quivered inwardly as if at a blow, but gave

him a shatteringly beautiful smile. 'Crude, Irvine, very crude.'

'But true.'

Mr Ducaine laughed, insensitive to his daughter's mortification or his wife's disapproval. 'And why not, I ask you? She's had to make do with the stereotyped scions of the winefarming nobility for six months now, and they're not really in her league. You must have seemed like the answer to a prayer, Kemp.'

'A maiden's prayer?' Kemp's eyes gleamed.

'Mother!' Emma breathed faintly, distressed.

'I don't think I approve of this sort of conversation,' Mrs Ducaine stated distastefully, rising to her daughter's appeal. 'I'm sure that now Miss McLaren knows your identity, Kemp, her attitude will change.'

'Will it, Valentine?' he asked sceptically.

Truthfully, she wasn't sure. 'Obviously, we'll be seeing a great deal of each other, so the answer to that will keep. Unless, of course, you're comtemplating firing me?'

'I must certainly consider that resort,' he countered smoothly. 'I hate to think what you're doing to Fleurmont's image. The main part of your job, I believe, brings you into contact with the visiting public. Most of the estates, as I recall, have nice girls like Emma in that particular rôle.'

Valentine couldn't fault that description of Emma, although the other girl didn't seem to like it much and looked unhappy. She was indeed a nice girl, an outdoor girl, the-girl-next-door, neither too overwhelmingly clever nor too boringly stupid, and she was pretty as well. Her hair, aristocratic-mouse, was always squeaky clean, and she wore it long and straight. Pink, sweet lips concealed good teeth, her eyes were clear and grey, and she had a good figure although her bones were heavier than Valentine's, and she was perhaps three inches shorter. She was actually a few months older than Valentine, but seemed much younger.

Valentine had frequently reflected on how much Emma

seemed to dislike her, and now, noticing the way she looked at Kemp Irvine, decided that prior knowledge of the man had been the cause. She felt a brief stirring of wistfulness. Emma was ideal material for an estate owner's wife. Would Kemp prove to be the typical estate owner? But surely he was a man apart. Was Emma rare and special enough for him?

'Valentine knows her job and does it well,' Mr Ducaine, who liked her, was speaking up for her.

'And as the prime requisite of any job is keeping the boss happy, I think I should be getting back to Fleurmont now,' Valentine said, looking at Kemp. 'How awful! You'll have arrived at the house and found no one there and no preparations for your return, except that Salome Jansen and Maude did go through the bedrooms with a duster and polisher this morning. I'm so sorry.'

'You're apologising for nothing,' he assured her. 'I haven't been to Fleurmont yet. I saw the lights from the main road as I passed here, realised a party was in progress and decided to gatecrash in the hope of encountering old friends and acquaintances. You were unexpected. You don't really fit in, do you, so it might be as well if you did make your departure now.'

It was a clear dismissal, and not a polite one, but she already knew he was a man who would eschew good manners when they might get in the way of his making his wishes known.

'Will I see you later, or tomorrow?' she asked.

'Oh, don't wait up, Valentine,' Emma advised, having apparently recovered some of her usual spirit, perhaps realising that Kemp seemed to dislike the other girl. 'We'll probably keep him here for ages yet.'

'Yes. Kemp is a very old friend of ours, you must understand,' Mrs Ducaine added distantly.

Valentine looked at her, the powdered and pampered product of the privileged society in which she had lived all her life, and understood very clearly. The plumply pretty older woman was repeating Kemp's suggestion that she didn't belong and could never do so, warning her to keep her distance. She felt a stirring of regret. Previously Mrs Ducaine had been friendly, and Valentine knew she was witnessing the surfacing of the age-old maternal instinct to defend the offspring's interests.

'I understand,' Valentine said coolly with a malicious little smile, determined not to reveal her hurt. 'I'll say goodnight, then, and go ... After I've seen your son Adam.'

Mrs Ducaine flushed angrily, but her husband laughed and Kemp looked amused, clearly divining her motive.

'He'll probably insist on driving you home,' Mr Ducaine said knowingly.

'I came in my own car,' Valentine explained, a dazzling smile encompassing them all. 'Goodnight everyone. Mr Irvine ... Kemp! I'll be seeing you.'

'I'll look forward to it,' he said urbanely, meaninglessly, and transferred his attention to Emma, who had hold of his arm by now, clinging to it as an affectionate child might do.

Valentine moved away from them, taking her time deliberately, her movements imbued with a delicately swaying grace, her pale flawless skin pearly under the soft artificial light that came from the trees.

Adam found her before she found him and she said goodnight, assuring him that she looked forward to seeing him again but skilfully managing to avoid making a definite date.

'I don't know what demands my boss will make on my time now that he's here,' she murmured vaguely.

She went through the same performance with Gary, whose parents had hosted the party, and let him accompany her to her white Escort Sports model.

Excitement was subsiding to a feeling of nervous anticipation of the future as she drove to Fleurmont with her window open to the summer night. Kemp Irvine filled her thoughts. Such a man—not the golden prince of a young girl's dreams, but a man; one she sensed could be cruel and often arrogant—but still such a man as she had waited for. Her self-awareness was such that she could recognise the richly passionate depths of her nature without flinching and, having a natural sense of her own worth as an individual human being, she knew she could never settle for less than would satisfy her. Nor could she ever be less than she was, playing the mouse when she had been born beautiful, and that was why Kemp Irvine hadn't been able to see through to the inner woman with all her doubts and uncertainties.

She had known, since the end of her schooldays, that all she had to do was wait, and one day she would see her mate and recognize him. In the meantime, she had intended to enjoy the waiting, and that first sadness, at seventeen, of being loved but unable to love in return had deterred her only briefly, for she had been young. It had taken the tragedy of Philip to crush her; to make her realise that the dating game, the flirtation game, could be dangerous when played by someone like herself. After that, the waiting had ceased to be fun. Once her wounds had closed over the inner, permanently throbbing pain of self-blame, she had sworn to avoid the nice men, the sensitive men she liked, such as poor Henry van Wyk tonight. Thus far she could and must go, out of consideration for others, but no farther. Being beautiful could be agonising, but she was defiant about remaining beautiful, making the most of her looks.

Tonight she had seen Kemp Irvine and perhaps the waiting was over. Only he didn't even like her, but once he knew her and understood what had happened to her ... oh, please, surely he would revise his opinion, for he was a highly intelligent man. But if he didn't—Valentine's mind skipped away from such an unbearable thought.

The Hattinghs' house, close to the entrance of the estate, was in complete darkness as she passed, so they would have to wait until tomorrow to know that Kemp Irvine had arrived. Driving at a lower speed now, Valentine approached the main buildings by way of the oak-lined drive. They were mighty trees, staunch and old, descendants of the original oaks planted in the Cape by Governor Simon van der Stel in the latter half of the seventeenth century, and they seemed to epitomise all the ancient graciousness of this region.

Time could hardly be said to have stood still here, but the way of life remained more leisurely and elegant than that to be found in the cities, even an old and beautiful one like Cape Town which Valentine loved. Here the good things abounded: it was a world of historic, beautifully perserved buildings; exquisite antique furniture which was lovingly cared for and in which people took a pride; a world of fine wines, clear fresh air, dogs and horses.

It came to her then that Kemp Irvine was a man of the present, even of the future, coming to this stiller, quieter way of life, and she wondered how he would adapt to it. There was a restlessness she had noticed in him earlier . . .

The estate dogs rushed to greet her as she parked her car in one of the garages, the red setter almost hysterical in his welcome, the Great Dane gentler in accordance with his placid nature, and they kept close beside her as she crossed the courtyard, pausing to look about her with fresh interest now that she knew the owner and wondering if he would find his inheritance a burden and wish to sell.

In the garden stood the old slave-bell, a much-needed reminder to the nostalgic that these were better days, and the three buildings were superb examples of Cape-Dutch architecture with their thatched roofs and exquisitely curved white gables. Younger than some of the buildings on neighbouring farms, they were still rich in history, the original living quarters, cellar and coach-house having been constructed in the late 1700s. The present wine cellar too, had been built before that century had given way to the next, but the existing main house was a mere hundred and sixty years old.

'Calm down, Rufus!' Valentine adjured the red setter. 'Why are you so neurotic?'

One of the Jansens would have fed the dogs earlier, but Valentine had been unacquainted with dogs until coming here and thus tended to spoil them, so she let them into the house with her and took them through to the kitchen.

'Although Salome will be cross if she finds out,' she murmured as she tossed them the titbits they had known she would provide.

She left them shut in the kitchen, deciding she needn't let them out until she went to bed, and then hesitated, wondering which bedroom Salome would have assigned to her new employer. The main one, probably. She had spent a long time in there that morning, but she wouldn't have made up the bed.

In all the six months she had been on Fleurmont, Valentine had never been inside that main bedroom. She was an intensely private person in many ways, and the value she placed on privacy had been increased with that soul-destroying invasion of her own privacy a year ago, when her name had been on everyone's lips and people had pointed at her in the streets, nudging their companions and some doing even worse than that. Thus she had shrunk fastidiously from intruding on that room where Fleurmont's previous owner and his wife had spent their married life.

Now, however, it was Kemp Irvine's room. Having collected sheets from the linen cupboard, she entered the room, confirmed that Salome had not made up the double bed and rapidly did so herself, removing blankets from the lovely old yellowwood chest which stood at its foot, concentrating on what she was doing yet, at the same time noticing and admiring the appointments of the large room. The furniture was of woods which were unobtainable these days, beautifully looked after, brilliantly polished.

Straightening up and briefly approving her work. Valentine turned away from the bed and her eyes fell on the tiny framed photograph that stood on the dressing-table.

'Philip!'

Her slim hand shook violently as she picked it up to make sure. She had made no mistake. Philip de Villiers looked out of the frame as he had looked at her in life, which soft dark eyes like a labrador's. The delicate features and curly brown hair were as she remembered them, and the sensitive mouth wore a dreamy smile which was something else she remembered.

The photograph clattered back on to the dressing-table top as Valentine bit back a cry of pure pain. For a moment she had been stunned enough to imagine, wildly, that the persecution was starting all over again, that someone had deliberately put the picture there to taunt her.

But it wasn't so. Philip's image stood there because it had a right to.

Pain, anguish, brought her to her knees and she knelt there on the thick soft rug, her arms crossed over her stomach where horror and tension became a gnawing torment, while the terrified blankness of her mind gave way to a spinning, frenzied chaos of thought. Karma, coincidence—could they be that cruel?

And the answer had to be that they could.

A hundred other questions clamoured for answer. Just how stupid had she been? How could she not have known? She couldn't even remember now if the lawyer had ever mentioned a name to her, or the Jansens or the Hattinghs. If they had, and it had been de Villiers, surely ... But Smith and Jones, Van der Merwe and Botha—de Villiers was almost as common.

Philip had never mentioned a wine-estate, yet surely only a son's photograph would stand in this main bedroom. If there had been no direct heir then Kemp Irvine's photograph would have had that place.

Dear God, Kemp Irvine ... Valentine tried to avoid the thought. It was too soon, she was too shocked, to think of the implications.

But—Philip's cousin?

And all the people she had come to know here, Philip's friends, or his parents'? Hadn't they realised who she was? Hadn't they remembered her name? Yet people were strangely obtuse at times and might not connect the Valli of a year ago with the Valentine they knew, while McLaren was ordinary enough and easily forgettable. Anyway, as friends of the family, they might have been sensitive enough to avoid the more sensational reports, the ones that had carried pictures of her.

And Kemp Irvine? Had he not made the connection either? He couldn't have. She had seen dislike and derision in those brilliant blue eyes, but not hatred. He had probably been out of South Africa at the time and had only heard about it all from Philip's parents, who might well have avoided her name altogether.

Valentine shuddered at a sudden memory of Reinette de Villiers, screaming at her, crazed by her hatred and grief for her son, while all around them flashbulbs exploded.

Resentment of the memory gave her strength and she rose to her feet. They had not been true, those words the woman had thrown at her before her husband pulled her away. She would never believe them.

She tilted her chin and glanced at her reflection in the mirror, automatically checking that her make-up did not need renewing. Her sapphire eyes were hard and bright, and her red mouth once again had the tight, bitter look of a year ago.

She would not be destroyed, she was promising herself as she left the room, but already her existence had become a world of suffering once more.

She went to the kitchen, realising that Kemp Irvine might arrive soon. He had been travelling a lot today and might be grateful if she left him some coffee in a flask.

Such a little service was all she could give him now, she realised poignantly, at last admitting the knowledge she had been avoiding.

She might have made him want her, understand her,

but once he knew who she was, and the part she had played in that old scandal, and she must tell him, he would feel nothing but hatred for her.

As she felt nothing but hatred for the fate which had played so cruelly with her.

Her head drooped a little on her slender white neck as she made the coffee, watched by Rufus and Chet. She forced herself to understand the situation and finally succeeded, killing hope just a few hours after it had been born.

CHAPTER TWO

'You may be a right royal bitch, but you've got the saddest mouth I've ever seen.'

Kemp Irvine's quiet voice roused Valentine from the reverie of acid-sharp memories into which she had fallen. She had brought her own cup of coffee into the sitting-room, accompanied by the dogs, and it had grown cold, untouched as she had given way to despair.

Rufus leapt to his feet, a torrent of nervous barks coming from him as he realised a stranger had intruded. Chet rose to his feet but waited for Valentine's reaction before committing himself.

'Quiet, Rufus!' she adjured, trying to gather some composure to her as she got to her feet. 'It's your new master. You'll have to make friends with Chet before he'll stop.'

'Temperamental?' he enquired, giving his attention to Chet.

'And very nervous.' As she felt, at that moment.

'His breed often are. Do they sleep indoors?'

'No. In fact, I'll let them out now,' Valentine volunteered, feeling the need to get out of his sight if only for a few seconds.

Judging by his initial remark, he was fully aware of having caught her in a vulnerable moment, and that, she instructed herself, must never happen again. You didn't share pain; you didn't show it.

The dogs accompanied her through the long hall with its glossy red-brown tiled floor, a typical feature of these old houses, and she let them out and locked the door, something she had not bothered to do while they were still with her.

When she returned to the sitting-room, her brightest smile was firmly in place, hiding the anguish that lay in her mind.

'Well, Mr Irvine?'

'Well, Miss McLaren? Were you waiting for me?'

'No.' In spite of herself, she couldn't resist adding, 'Are you disappointed?'

'No,' he countered, but he looked sceptical, for which she could hardly blame him, considering her attitude earlier that evening. 'Are you disappointed that I'm not?'

She shook her head, maintaining her smile with an effort. 'I wasn't expecting you as early as this after what Emma and Mrs Ducaine had to say.'

'It's after one, you know.'

Valentine glanced at the silver carriage clock above the fireplace and then at the cup of coffee she had forgotten.

'Night thoughts,' she murmured dismissively, looking at him from beneath shadows cast by long dark eyelashes. 'You are, of course, the boss, but I'm not on duty at this hour, so unless there's anything particular you want to know . . .?'

'All questions can be asked tomorrow,' he stated. 'I'm not in the mood for thinking of this Fleurmont business tonight.'

She remembered that he had been travelling and noticed that there were lines of fatigue bracketing his mouth.

'Tomorrow, then,' she confirmed. 'However, I do have one question to ask now, if you don't mind: what was your uncle's name?'

'Edward de Villiers.' His eyebrows rose. 'Why? It sounds important.'

Perhaps a fragment of hope had remained, but it died now, although she was careful not to betray the sudden deep weariness that pervaded her being.

'I just wondered,' she said lightly. 'I don't think anyone

ever mentioned it to me and I assumed it was Irvine.'

'My mother was his sister,' he informed her briefly.

'Yes. Well, I'll say goodnight, then.' She turned towards the door, afraid that her despair wasn't quite under control. 'By the way, I've left you a flask of coffee if you want it and I've made up your bed.'

His lips twisted into an ironic smile as she glanced back. 'You won't share it with me, Valentine?'

She turned completely to face him at that. 'You don't mean the coffee, do you?'

'I don't.'

With an effort that wrenched her inwardly, she achieved a demure smile, shaking her shining dark head. 'We've only just met, darling.'

'The newness of our acquaintance didn't appear to be worrying you earlier tonight,' Kemp murmured, moving towards her, questing eyes travelling from the perfect bone structure of her face to the pale gleam of her bare right shoulder. 'You made it very clear then just what it was that you wanted, so what's changed?'

'I have,' she said tautly, her eyes bitter.

'You were also very direct then, which you're not being now,' he continued thoughtfully. 'I wonder why? It can't be the discovery that I'm your employer, because it wasn't then that the change took place ... Or are you one of those women who promise everything and then withhold fulfilment of that promise? There's a name for that type, Valentine.'

'I'm aware of it, but it doesn't apply to me,' she snapped. Calmer, she added, 'Anyway, I'm not sure if you really do know what it was I wanted, Kemp.'

'I know what it was,' he contradicted her softly. 'This! Right, Valentine?'

His left hand closed over her right shoulder and Valentine stood very still, scarcely breathing. Her face was a still mask, but a wild, terrible excitement, mixed with anguished regret, tore at her inwardly as she felt the long fingers move caressingly against her flesh.

'You're quite wrong, you know,' she assured him with deceptive composure.

'Am I?' His smile wasn't kind. 'You knew what you were inviting—no, begging for—with the attitude you adopted at the party.'

'Perhaps I was drunk,' Valentine suggested with a faint smile.

'You're too intelligent to allow yourself to become drunk, my lady.'

'Then, simply, I've changed my mind. It's my prerogative to do so, after all. I am a woman.' But, dear God, she hadn't changed it, and it was a hurt worse than anything that had gone before to pretend that she had.

'All woman. Glamorous and lovely and desirable—and available, as you made very clear earlier.' He laughed harshly and she realised anew just how tired he was. 'Ah, God! Here I am where I've little wish to be ... You'll have to be my consolation, Valentine.'

Here where he had little wish to be ... and but for her and the part she had played, he might not be here. Fleurmont would belong to Philip. Valentine knew she ought to tell him who she was, but the coward spirit begged for just a little longer, just a little time in which to experience, just this once, his arms about her and his lips on hers, because when he knew the truth he would never wish to touch her again.

It was self-indulgence, but she would never have any more of him. Her voice had dropped and contained a silvery, shivery quality as she asked slowly, 'Would I, could I, make it all worthwhile, then, Kemp?'

'Hardly.' His face was unyielding, his voice too. He would grant her nothing. 'You haven't that sort of power, sweetheart, but you could help me to forget for an hour or two.'

That would never have been enough for her. If only she had had more time. If only. She wanted to sob, to curse the cruel coincidence that had done this to her, but instead she kept her expression immobile and her face was like something carved of marble as she waited.

The hand on her shoulder stirred and slid around to the back of her neck beneath the silky cluster of dark curls, forcing her to tilt her head back while her lashes fluttered down over sapphire eyes in which the pupils had become dilated.

Suddenly disliking the sensation of having pitifully little control over herself or the situation, Valentine tried to quell the throbbing sense of anticipation which was violating her composure. He would kiss her and confirm what she had recognised at her first sight of him, but that was all. This excitement was an overreaction—and pointless. She knew now that she could never be anything in Kemp Irvine's life, and the knowledge was like a fresh wound added to all the other old ones.

Yet when his lips descended on hers it was like nothing she had ever known. For timeless moments she remained as still as a statue, waiting for the shock to subside, but the lightning darts of sensation flickering through her veins were gaining in strength, becoming both pain and pleasure.

And yet, she thought wonderingly, his hand at the back of her neck and his mouth exploring hers were the only parts of him that were touching her.

The pitch of her arousal gained an intolerable height all at once and an inarticulate murmur came from her throat as her body arched violently towards his, seeking closer contact. Instantly Kemp's arms came round her, gathering her rigid body up against him while his kisses deepened and Valentine discovered just how sensuous his mouth was.

There was a vibrant intensity in the closeness of their bodies, a straining after something more, closer and deeper and greater, something altogether more than this present hunger which locked their mouths together. Valentine felt her hips powerfully caressed as he propelled her still closer to him, and when his mouth was removed from hers she was gasping.

'Shall I undress you, or is stripping part of your act?' Kemp asked harshly. 'I'm sure you disrobe quite delightfully.'

'No.' Her voice was unusually husky, but a measure of sanity had returned to her, along with a reinforced awareness of what he could have meant to her. Ah, but how could life be so cruel?

'No?' His hands, sensitive, strong hands, caressed her slender waist. 'This is what you wanted, isn't it?'

'No,' she reiterated more clearly, opening her eyes and turning their blue blaze on his face.

One hand moved up from her waist to close over a taut breast. Her kiss-stung lips parted as a choked cry escaped her and the quivering ache in the base of her stomach became unbearable.

'My mind doesn't want it,' she qualified voluntarily, protest and pleasure mingling in her shaken voice.

'Sex has nothing to do with the intellect, sweetheart,' Kemp taunted.

'But it was never just sex that I wanted, you see,' she murmured, swaying slightly, and then wondered at her own stupid honesty. To have him know of her pain would only increase her vulnerability. Oh, at any price she must hide that from him.

'What then?' he enquired, removing his hands from her, and the severance of contact left her icy cold—but clearheaded.

'Something of a more long-term nature,' she confessed with her best and brightest smile, but it cost her dearly to speak the truth and still conceal its accompanying torment.

'Ah! The directness has returned,' he commented and there was cruelty in his intense gaze as he added mockingly, 'I'm afraid your suit is hopeless, Miss McLaren.'

'I'm afraid it is,' she agreed lightly, putting up a slim hand to smooth her hair and noticing that it shook slightly. 'I won't even ask for permission to hope. Anyway, as I said earlier, I've changed my mind.'

'Thank God for that,' he returned sardonically. 'You're not built for the longer distances, angel, only for sprints . . . In the heat of a passionate moment you could devastate, but I'd hate to live with you.'

Contemptuous blue eyes glittered over her exquisite face, lingering on her throbbing lips which were swollen by his long kisses and denuded of every vestige of lipstick. Valentine forced another brittle smile. She ought to tell him of her connection with Philip now, she knew, but she felt suddenly lethargic, tired deep into her bones. Tomorrow—tomorrow would do.

'Kemp?'

He shook his head, looking back at her disgustedly. 'Forget it. Suddenly that flask of coffee you mentioned seems infinitely more appealing than you do . . . Unless, of course, you're prepared to tell me just what sort of game it is that you're playing?'

'Does it have to be a game?' she retaliated icily, strengthened by his open contempt. 'I find I've made a mistake, that's all. You'd be doing me a favour if you refrained from referring to it again.'

'Now why in the world should I want to do you a favour?' he drawled.

Valentine couldn't resist it. Soon, she realised anguishedly, he would not permit her to even address him, let alone flirt. In all probability he would send her away from Fleurmont. Her eyes went limpid and her tone was honeyed as she murmured, 'Most men do.'

'As you yourself pointed out earlier, I'm not most men,' he reminded her. 'I'm not even like them. Most men would soon find themselves ensnared in your mesh, totally confused by your advance-and-retreat tactics. As it is, I'm merely wondering if perhaps the meringue metaphor wasn't apt after all.'

'A hollow woman?' she queried, and hoped she succeeded in hiding her bitterness.

'Well, are you?' Kemp prompted abruptly. 'Beneath the wiles and the artifice—is there anything there at all, Valentine?'

'You might find out,' she suggested sweetly.

'I don't think I can be bothered. I saw clearly just what you were from the moment I set eyes on you, and nothing has caused me to revise my opinion.'

'Yet you will,' she promised him in liquid tones, and wondered bitterly if he would recall her words when she told him the truth. And then. 'I am—me. I can see, I can feel that you despise me for that. But why should I be other than I am? That would be a betrayal, a denial, of what God or nature granted me.'

'Words,' he retorted dismissively. 'They're an intrinsic part of your remarkable act and you use them well, but they don't mean anything, do they? Why don't you go away to your bed? I've been travelling all day and I can do without your silly little sorties at this hour of the night.'

Valentine glanced at the clock and was surprised to see how much time had passed since she had last done so.

'I'm sorry,' she said. 'Goodnight, Kemp.'

'Really goodnight this time?' he enquired hopefully.

'It was you who delayed my departure last time I said it,' she reminded him with a faint, delicate smile, and drifted from the room, for the ability to move silently was just one of the many arts comprising the whole that was Valentine.

The encounter had drained her, for every word had been an effort. She was tired and a prey to countless regrets, but she still took infinite care over the removal of her make-up and had a shower, grateful for the fact that an adjoining bathroom had been added to her bedroom at some recent time, since she felt unable to face a further encounter with Kemp that night.

Finally she went through the rest of her nightly beauty routine, for she valued her appearance, however much she hated the often disastrous effects of her beauty.

In bed she lay awake, still endeavouring to fully reconcile herself to the knowledge that she could hope for nothing from Kemp Irvine. It made bitter knowing, when she also knew that could she only have met him without armour, as her true self, she might, given time, have altered his present opinion of her. But the fact of his being Philip's cousin had put an end to that. She would need to be constantly acting, concealing hurt.

She thought about him for a long time, reliving his long kisses, seeing his face, hearing his voice, and the intensity of her absorption brough a fresh fear to her. She had thought of him earlier that here was a man whom she could never bring to his knees, a prime requisite as far as she was concerned, but now she wondered—could he do that to her, have her at his feet and then trample over her?

Yet though she thought of Kemp so long before sleep came, it was of Philip that she dreamed, experiencing again their first meeting in distorted, nightmarish fashion, and when she woke up with her heart hammering in fear, she forced herself to relive it yet again, as it had really been. They had met, unromantically enough, in a public library, both reaching for *Martin Chuzzlewit*, and the admiration for Dickens they had both confessed had been just the first of many discoveries of common interests.

Their mutual tastes regarding the arts had been the sole basis for their relationship, as Valentine had later realised, blaming herself for not seeing more clearly. She had gradually come to feel a certain affection for the young man without ever realising what was happening where his own emotions had been concerned. She had been too absorbed in the programme of films and plays they chose to attend, or else she hadn't cared sufficiently, to wonder why he seemed to have no background to his life. Parents and childhood were never mentioned and she

hadn't asked about them. Nor, in those days, had she had
the wisdom to enquire about a man's marital status. She
had taken it for granted that he was single. Young—she
had been young and stupid. Never again.

Thus far did her thoughts take her before she slept
again, but always fitfully.

In some dark despairing hour of that restless night she
took a decision to resign from her post at Fleurmont, but
by the time Maude, the Black domestic servant who
helped Mrs Jansen in the house, brought her morning
coffee, Valentine was in a defiant mood. She had run
away from Cape Town, but she could not go on running
for ever. To fail to win was one thing; to be actively
defeated quite another. She must endure Kemp's contempt which would surely turn to hatred when she told
him the truth. It would be agony, she knew, but to run
again was out of the question. The one thing she could
never escape from was herself. She was what she was, and
she couldn't change that because she refused to. The spirit
died when forced into an alien shape, its natural in-
clinations suppressed.

She donned another white dress, a sundress this time,
of fine, very soft cotton over which she wore a matching
sleeveless jacket with bright Madeira-work at the shoulders and a drawstring at the waist. She spent a long
time at her make-up since there were shadows to be
concealed beneath her eyes, and she parted her hair in
the centre and drew it back from her face, a style which
suited her since it fully exposed her high cheekbones,
but at the back of her head the romantic dark curls
were left free.

Finally, slipping on high-heeled sandals, she went along
to the large breakfast room to find the table set for two.
The windows stood wide open and she crossed to them,
breathing the sweet clean air of a summer morning while
her eyes went to the lower slopes of the surrounding
mountains where a host of pale yellow wild flowers spread
in a great shining sheet. Freddie Jansen, the husband of

the housekeeper and also a Fleurmont employee, had
told her that they had bloomed there of their own
accord every summer for as long as anyone could remember, and it was probably from them that the estate
had derived its name.

Salome Jansen bustled in with a bowl of fruit and the
coffee pot.

'So, the new boss man has arrived, hey?' she said in her
quick birdlike voice as Valentine turned to smile at her.
'Last night, he said.'

'Yes. I saw him then.'

'He's a man, that one,' Salome commented briefly, and
didn't explain what she meant by that, but Valentine
knew. 'Though I must say, he doesn't seem too pleased to
be here.'

'No. Well, I suppose it has been rather forced on him
in a way,' Valentine suggested carefully.

'True. Perhaps he'll sell.' Salome paused. 'Well, I must
get on. He says he wants to have the Hattinghs up here
for dinner tonight, so I've a menu to plan. It'll be good
for Fleurmont to entertain again—the dust was starting
to settle.'

She left the room as hurriedly as she had entered it, a
plump, brisk woman whose hair was dyed a startling
shade of amber.

Valentine poured herself a cup of coffee and returned
to the window. Just what changes would Fleurmont's
reluctant owner bring about? She looked out at the scene
which could still hold her attention after six months: there
were the horses, a black and two grey mares, waiting for
Freddie to come to them, and tiny Binnie Hattingh had
already made her way up from the other house in search
of her friend Trevor Jansen and they were running about
with the dogs, Binnie's silvery fairness contrasting with
Trevor's darkness.

Two larger figures appeared, and Valentine felt her
stomach muscles contract at the sight of Kemp Irvine,
tall and lithe, with the sun making his light brown hair

look fair. Beside him was Freddie Jansen, and Valentine felt amused as she noted that for once his crumpled, Walter Matthau-type face wore a broad beaming smile.

'Congratulations,' she said mockingly a few minutes later when Kemp entered the breakfast room. She was determined to start this new day without revealing weakness. 'For the last six months Freddie Jansen has grumbled constantly about your non-appearance and now, when you finally arrive, he's instantly on your side.'

'On my side?' Kemp tested the words thoughtfully as he accepted a cup of coffee from her and sat down. 'Is there a war on, then?'

Valentine regarded him contemplatively with her head tilted slightly, her sapphire eyes sparkling as she registered the challenge which touched her pain even as she admired it.

'Quite possibly,' she conceded, and smiled.

'But tell me then, Valentine, who is the aggressor?'

She arched a delicate eyebrow. 'Whichever one is in the position of strength, surely?'

'Who is?' he prompted, looking amused.

'Ah, well . . .' She lowered her eyes to the table, deliberately flirtatious, but the answer to his question frightened her. 'I feel it would be diplomatic not to speculate about that, darling.'

'Or else you prefer not to admit the truth,' he guessed tauntingly. 'Do you always bestow endearments on all and sundry?'

'You're not exactly all and sundry, are you?' she countered truthfully.

He leaned back, watching her with idle interest. 'You're really quite remarkable, aren't you?' he commented quietly. 'Are you always this bright and beautiful at breakfast?'

'Always. I pride myself on it.'

'Our visitors must adore you.'

'Sales of wine on the estate have escalated since I came

here,' she said mischievously, but wondered if she was succeeding in hiding her pain—or did he guess at the rawness within her and wonder at its cause?

'Conceited too,' he mocked. 'You're on duty from when?'

'Nine. But today being Saturday, I finish work at lunchtime.' Valentine paused before confiding. 'When I first came I was amazed to learn that we're closed to the public on Saturday afternoons and Sundays, since one imagines that those are the times when most people are likely to get into their cars and drive out into the Boland. But since none of the other estates welcomes the public at those times, there'd be no point in our doing so.'

'You see, on so many of the estates your job is done by the owner's wife or daughters and if they kept such hours they wouldn't be able to enjoy any sort of relaxation in their own homes,' Kemp explained.

'As it is, we get the occasional people who haven't read the information turning up out of hours,' Valentine told him. 'Anyway, even with the short hours, the whole business seems to have gone from strength to strength since its inception in the early seventies. We get local people and tourists calling.'

'You sound like a brochure—is that what your job entails?'

'I have to be available to our visitors, to conduct tours through the production cellar, although those who prefer it can stroll through on their own,' she began. 'I also pour the wine for those who wish to taste; I handle the sales on the estate; and I must be able to answer questions about simply everything—what to look for when tasting, the soil, climate, cultivars, the whole process of wine production and I must have a knowledge of Fleurmont's architectural history and the furniture on display in the room where they taste and buy.'

'And was all the requisite knowledge already inside that pretty head of yours when you came here?'

'What I didn't know, Sylvie and James Hattingh taught

me, but we're a Cape family, so we always had wine at home,' she explained.

'The other provinces are catching up with us,' Kemp commented. 'In fact, South Africa has become more and more a wine-drinking country in recent years.'

'A trend that's not going to change while prices remain as reasonable as they are now,' Valentine suggested.

'Where is home, incidentally?'

'Gordon's Bay.'

'An attractive town. I used to go to the yacht club there. Have you always lived there?'

'Until I went to U.C.T. at seventeen.'

'You've a degree?'

'Not a hollow woman after all, you see,' she challenged. 'Plus, I have secretarial skills. I wasn't sure exactly what my majors, English and Industrial Psychology, would equip me for, so I spent my vacations getting extra qualifications.'

'I'm surprised you found the time,' Kemp drawled. 'I rather visualise you as being so involved in the social side of varsity life that you'd have failed to get your degree. Surely you must have been Rag Queen at some stage?'

'I didn't go in for that sort of thing,' Valentine said.

His lips twisted into the ironic smile that was becoming familiar. 'Modesty or reserve? Or that conceit I mentioned just now—you didn't need any confirmation of your beauty? I suspect you're singularly arrogant, Valentine.'

'As you are.' She knew it was unwise and that she was inviting for herself the pain of rejection, but she timed her pause perfectly. 'We make a good pair.'

'We're not a pair—yet,' he added meaningly, and Valentine knew in that moment that, much as he still disliked her, he meant to have her. 'But, my dear girl, all your qualifications are quite wasted on your present work. Even your secretarial skills aren't required, since Sylvie Hattingh apparently handles the office work. What brought you out here, away from Cape Town which, I would say, is your natural element?'

It was an opening for her to tell him the truth, but something in her cried out against doing so. Not yet, oh, not just yet. Let her have just a little longer before she must see the hatred in his eyes. She had derived bitter-sweet pleasure from their encounter this morning and he had listened when she had described her work, so . . . Just a little longer.

Kemp was watching her intently as he waited for her answer and she wondered if she had inadvertently betrayed her inward dilemma. To keep on acting, con-cealing, was so difficult, when all she yearned for was rest; the support and strength he might have given to a woman he cared about.

'What was it, Valentine?' he prompted impatiently. 'The knowledge that the wine-producing districts abound in wealthy and eligible young men like Adam Ducaine?'

She met his eyes. Here at least was a truth she could give him. 'Whatever other descriptions may be applied to me, mercenary isn't one of them.'

'I believe you,' he said surprisingly, but his tone was far from friendly. 'Your interests lie in other directions, don't they? And some of those other adjectives that may be applied to you are far less flattering than mercenary. So—what brought you out here?'

'You're condemning me for being myself again,' she said flatly, an inner ache flawing her act. 'Should I creep around like a little brown mouse because my true image makes people distrust me? Oh, let's just say I like the life here.'

Kemp looked disbelieving. 'Emma was telling me that you don't appear to have adapted at all well.'

Regretful envy quivered through her. Emma had no past to destroy her dreams. Still Valentine managed a smile. 'I'd forgotten Emma. I wonder why she hasn't come rushing over yet to make sure I'm keeping my hands off you. It's quite late already . . . In fact, I'd better get over to the cellar. I like to make sure I've got enough of everything before people start arriving.'

Kemp rose with her. 'I'll accompany you. I went around most areas with Freddie Jansen before breakfast, but I haven't seen your particular province yet.'

They crossed the short distance between the house and cellar in silence. Distantly the voices of Binnie and Trevor could be heard, punctuated by barks from Rufus. A few people were about now, going about their business, and Valentine smiled at those employees she knew.

Maude was already in the room, attached to the cellar, where Valentine had her dealings with the public.

'Enough glasses, Maude?' she asked.

'Yes, miss.'

'People pocket them as souvenirs,' she explained to Kemp. 'Some of the estates charge for them and then people can take them away openly.'

Maude finished filling a jar with bread cubes for those connoisseurs who liked to cleanse their palates before moving on to taste the next wine.

'Everything all right, miss?'

Valentine ran an eye round the room, checking that the beautiful hand-crafted furniture which had survived centuries was dust-free and shining.

'Yes, thank you, Maude.'

Maude departed and Valentine looked at Kemp.

'And these?' He indicated a pile of printed diagrams.

'Maps of the production cellar illustrating the entire process from the moment the grapes go into the crusher right through to the labelling of the certified wines,' she explained. 'A lot of people prefer to wander through on their own, and these assist them.'

'A good idea.' He seemed restless and his eyes went to the antique corking machine displayed in one corner. 'I remember that. I was with Edward when he discovered it. Ah, well, I'd better be getting over to the office as Hattingh should be arriving soon.'

The strange reluctance with which he spoke brought a

new dimension to what Valentine understood of him.
Here was a highly complex man whose needs and values
were different to those held by other more ordinary men.

'You really do hate being here, don't you?' she
ventured, following him to the door and stepping out into
the sunshine again.

His eyes went to the acres of vineyards and the flower-
starred lower slopes of the mountains, and she guessed
that where she saw beauty, he was seeing boundaries that
trapped.

'I neither expected nor wanted this burden, for that's
all it amounts to.' He glanced at her. 'Strange as it
probably seems to you. I can't expect you to understand.'

'I think I do.' Valentine hesitated, then continued.
'You've lived a different sort of life, one that obviously
attracted you or why else would you have chosen it? I've
seen most of your documentaries on television, certainly
the ones exploring and exposing various facets of the
human condition and the deprivations brought about by
either social or political influences. I know that they can
only have been made by someone totally committed to
his task. Obviously you'll find Fleurmont different and
probably restrictive.'

His eyes scanned her still face, seeking something, conviction perhaps.

'You're obviously an intelligent woman, Valentine.' His
voice grew harsher as he went on. 'You'll have to excuse
me if I'm not as appreciative as you deserve. I've a pre-
judice against clever, beautiful women. It's thanks to one
such, a brilliant and beautiful bitch by all accounts, that
I'm here today and the owner of this estate.'

There was a silent scream torturing her mind as
something died in her heart. She had never felt so bereft,
so hopeless.

'A woman?' she queried through stiff lips.

'A woman,' he ground out. 'I don't suppose you'll know
this since people around here avoid referring to it—the
whole sordid business only happened about a year ago. I

was in Mauritania at the time and only heard about it
after it was all over. Edward and Reinette had a son,
Philip—my cousin. He was ten years younger than me.
He took his life after this . . . this super-bitch had caused
him to break up his marriage with her promises and then
arbitrarily changed her mind.'

'Perhaps . . . perhaps she didn't know he was married,'
Valentine got out tonelessly.

He cast her a contemptuous glance. 'Women always
know.'

But she hadn't, she hadn't! It was still vivid in her
memory, an endless pain, that moment when Philip had
uttered the words 'my wife'.

'And his wife?' she asked, keeping her face expressionless
with difficulty. She had always wanted to know what had
become of the woman whom she regarded as the true
victim of what Kemp so rightly described as a sordid
affair.

'Rose?'

Valentine knew the name before he said it. In the midst
of her horror at Philip's revelation had come that moment
of cruelly ironic coincidence when he had mentioned his
wife's name, for Rose was also her own second name.

'Philip was a bloody fool, no woman is worth that, but
it's Rose I'm sorry for,' Kemp went on. He shook his
head. 'My God, it's as if a curse had been laid on the
family! First that, and then six months later Edward and
Reinette were killed in that accident, and here am I, left
with all this which I simply do not want.'

'You could sell.' She must keep responding or he would
sense something wrong. She ought to tell him now, but
she couldn't. To do so would require greater courage than
she had at her command at that moment.

'But could I?' Once more his restless gaze swept the
vineyards. 'This, Fleurmont, meant everything to Edward
and Reinette to whom I owe much of the security I had
in my youth; its staying in the family meant so much to
them . . . Our Chenin Blanc, Edward's greatest pride, was

named for his wife, La Reine, and he and Philip used to talk about adding a Rosé to our list and naming it for Rose.'

'I hadn't known that—the origin of the Chenin Blanc's lovely name.' Valentine was responding automatically, while her mind fought the despair that rose like a flood tide, threatening to immerse her completely.

'Something for you to tell the romantics among our visitors,' Kemp suggested with biting humour. His expression was so implacable that Valentine felt the blood freeze in her veins. 'God! Sometimes I feel I'd like to go after the woman who did that to my cousin. I'd take her and break her, destroying her the way she destroyed him. Believe me, she'd never be whole again!'

CHAPTER THREE

SITTING down to lunch with Kemp after a busy morning, Valentine knew she was living on borrowed time—no, stolen time. Because she ought to have told him the truth this morning. Self-disgust made her taunt herself with accusations of cowardice. Tonight, she promised silently, after James and Sylvie had gone; then she would tell him.

Sipping her Riesling, which was the product of another estate, not their own, she thought to ask, 'Will you decide what wine you want for tonight ... Incidentally, I am assuming that I'll be joining you, or is that presumptuous?'

'You live here as well, don't you?' he dismissed the question. 'You'd be an asset to any social occasion as you're probably aware. I'll have to ask Salome what the menu is.'

'We've a number of wines from other estates in our private stock,' she ventured.

Kemp smiled. 'I think we'd better make use of Fleurmont's, since it's our own cellarmaster we'll be entertaining. Incidentally, which of our wines are most popular among the visitors who come to taste and buy?'

'All of them,' Valentine stated promptly.

'Ah! A loyal employee,' he laughed. 'Relax, Valentine, I'm not thinking of firing you.'

But after he heard what she had to say tonight, he might do so, she thought bitterly. She could hardly blame him either.

'Seriously, though,' she continued, 'obviously the Chenin Blanc leads the field, but the Tinta Barocca and Cabernet Sauvignon are equally famous, having been awarded prizes both locally and overseas. But the Shiraz

43

sells well too, and the Cinsaut is very popular, especially with women and the younger men who haven't yet acquired a taste for the heavier reds. It's my personal favourite, along with La Reine.'

Adam Ducaine arrived before they had finished the light meal which they were eating out of doors.

'Too early, am I?' he asked casually as he bent to kiss the satiny cheek Valentine offered to him. 'Are you coming to watch polo?'

She gave him a small smile, thinking tiredly that since she would never be anything in Kemp's life, she might as well continue to project a frivolous attitude towards Adam. 'Need you ask, darling? Don't I always watch? The only unpredictable bit about it all is who'll get here first to invite me.' She turned to Kemp, catching his amused glance. 'I'm off duty, or are you changing my hours?'

'I'm playing polo myself,' he informed her. 'Adam's father arranged it last night. He and Adam and me and—who else?'

'Gary or his father, I expect, and the opposing team is from the same crowd,' Adam supplied. His eyes returned to Valentine with flattering rapidity. 'Edward's ponies have remained stabled at the club, as I think you know. Only the best players have been allowed to ride them, Kemp. That doesn't include me, I'm afraid.'

'Are you a good player, Kemp?' Valentine asked guilelessly, and wondered painfully what punishment was in store for her when he knew the truth and remembered her attitude now.

'Yes,' he said simply, looking entertained by her manner.

'Best handicap around here,' Adam added reluctantly. 'We're all dreading being shown up this afternoon.'

Adam left his car at Fleurmont and they drove to the club in Kemp's new silver Porsche which he was still running in. When they arrived at the club, people stared at them as they strolled to the pavilion and not just because Kemp was newly returned to the district. They made a startlingly attractive and elegant pair, the man almost fair-haired, but tanned and very tall, and the girl, not quite as tall, a fragile, willowy creature whose beauty was almost shocking even with dark glasses concealing her eyes.

A gentle breeze moulded the soft skirt of her dress against her long legs and she walked beside Kemp with unselfconscious grace, her red lips curved into a lovely smile which blended delight and amusement and completely hid her inner misery. She felt proud to be seen with him, quite forgetting Adam at her other side. She would have liked to tuck her hand through Kemp's arm, just to reinforce everyone's awareness that they were together, but an inherent instinct for the natural perimeters of public behaviour made her refrain. Anyway, she had no right to do it, she thought sadly.

Kemp must have been aware of the attention they were attracting as well, because he glanced at her, read the meaning of her smile and murmured, 'You're enjoying yourself, aren't you?'

'Yes,' she agreed candidly, and her smile became even more meltingly lovely, though without the dark glasses she might have seemed wistful. 'Everyone is looking at us.'

'Exhibitionist!' he taunted. For a moment his eyes rested on her face, hardening slightly, then he spoke across her, addressing Adam. 'Will Emma be here?'

'I imagine she'll be over just as soon as she can,' Adam assured him. 'But she was late getting back ... For some obscure reason she suddenly took it into her head to go down to Cape Town this morning, a spur-of-the-moment decision. I was left to take over her job and handle our visitors. Did that party of Americans come to Fleurmont as well, Valentine?'

He wanted her attention and she gave it to him reluctantly for a few seconds. Beside Kemp, Adam and all the other men here were . . . tame.

When the game in which they were playing began, she watched with more interest than she usually felt, simply because Kemp was playing. Even in the regulation polo gear, which she had always thought somewhat unattractive, he was a figure to draw attention.

As she might have expected, he played at number three. It was somehow characteristic that he should occupy that vital position where his task was both to open attacks and support the number four, Mr Ducaine, in defence. Each of the mounts he used, changing after every two chukkas, was highly trained and the game was played at lightning speed.

Again, watching him, Valentine felt pride mingling with her sadness. Even now it seemed as if he was somehow part of her. His presence on the field was commanding and he was far and away the best player among the eight.

But she still wondered if this sort of life, dictated by the cycle of wine-producing but nevertheless attended by plentiful leisure and pleasure, could ever truly satisfy him. The life he had previously led must have tempered him, making him aware of things of which those who stayed at home were ignorant, and all this might not be enough to fulfil him when the gift which had made him respected was far from being fully expanded.

Someone sat down beside her and Valentine turned her head reluctantly, feeling momentarily perturbed when she beheld Emma Ducaine, neat and pretty in a pale blue linen dress and white sandals. Then she thought with sudden defiance—she was damned if she was going to let Emma know that she was no real rival to her.

'Oh, good,' Emma said with relief. 'I thought I might be too late to see Kemp play.'

'Aren't you interested in the fortunes of your father and brother at all?' Valentine asked naughtily, irrationally determined to provoke, as if by upsetting Emma she might alleviate some of her own pain.

Emma blushed. 'Them too, of course. But Kemp . . . I haven't seen him for years. How is he playing?'

'Quite brilliantly,' Valentine had no hesitation in responding. Let Emma think she was being challenged! 'But then I imagine he does everything brilliantly.'

Emma looked at her curiously, but Valentine was watching the game again, and anyway, her eyes were safely secret behind sunglasses.

'You like him, don't you?' Emma queried.

'Like?' Valentine felt as if a knife twisted in her heart, but she gave the girl an assessing glance. She knew she was being perverse, but she didn't care. If she gave up the game, she might fall to pieces, and above all, Emma was someone she didn't want looking at her essentially private agony. 'An insipid word, Emma, or were you employing it as a euphemism?'

'I don't know what you mean.' Emma watched the game for a few moments—or rather, she watched Kemp, hungrily. Then, 'How are you getting on with him? Has he come to a decision about whether you're to keep your job?'

If he hadn't decided to fire her yet, he would when he knew the truth, Valentine thought bleakly. But with a faint laugh, she said, 'Don't you think he was only joking when he said he must consider the possibility of firing me?'

'I didn't think so,' Emma said stiffly.

'Perhaps your sense of humour is of a different brand to Kemp's . . . and mine,' Valentine suggested limpidly, but it cost her considerable effort. She thought achingly—it's probably true, but you have more chance than me because there's no Philip in your past.

'You don't understand . . . You hardly know him, Valentine.' Emma muttered rebelliously.

'In the sense you mean, but in another sense I feel as if I've known him since the beginning of time,' Valentine told her mischievously, keeping her voice light, wishing fervently that the girl would go away. She wanted to be alone with her ever-increasing pain. 'Have you ever heard of that happening, Emma? Seeing someone for the first time and in that same instant recognising them, as if you'd known each other in a previous life?'

'You're imagining things,' Emma responded brusquely. 'How . . . how can you even begin to know and understand a man like Kemp? You . . . you don't belong here, you don't fit in!'

'What are you getting so upset for?' Valentine enquired interestedly. Please God, she hid her own gnawing distress better than Emma did hers.

Flushing, Emma subsided, muttering ungraciously. Valentine watched the conclusion of the game which ended in victory for Kemp's side. She wondered if Emma's unhappiness came anywhere close to hers in intensity. Why did women have to be so weak, so dependent on men for happiness?

Then, determined to play to the finish of her own game, whatever it cost her in terms of pain and effort, she turned to Emma and picked up her last words. 'Come to that, if you think about it, Kemp doesn't really belong here either.'

'What do you mean? Of course he belongs.'

'He comes from a different world, Emma,' Valentine said gently.

'He belongs to Fleurmont now,' Emma insisted obstinately.

'But have you seen the restlessness in his eyes?'

'He'll adjust, he'll settle down,' Emma predicted eagerly. 'Or he will, if you don't influence him into selling.'

Valentine was silent until the waiter bringing them cold drinks had departed. She felt filled with regret for what might have been. 'Who could influence Kemp Irvine, Emma?' she asked finally and knew it was the truth. Not she, not Emma, not anyone. 'It would be folly to try.'

'You'd try, though,' Emma accused heatedly. 'I know what it is, Valentine. You want him for yourself and because you're a city person you'd try to get him away from here.'

'Oh the contrary, I could enjoy this sort of living for the rest of my days, the luxury and the peace,' Valentine told her truthfully, and decided to go on with the truth. Somehow it eased her own pain to build fear in this girl's mind. 'And yes, I do want Kemp, but a man such as he is ... It's the duty of people like you and me not to stand in his way, Emma. How long can he be happy here?'

Emma's pretty pink lips quivered and Valentine realised that she was close to tears and felt sorry for her. It was better than feeling sorry for herself, and she had come close to that last night and today.

'Don't you know it's bad manners to be as honest as you've been about what you want, Valentine?' Emma said spitefully.

Valentine lifted her chin proudly. 'Why should I dissemble?' she asked with a tight little smile.

'You'll never get him.'

The knife twisted again. Why did the truth always have to be so agonising? She hoped desperately that the other girl wasn't perceptive enough to realise what those cruel little words had done to her. However resolutely she sustained her gruelling act, surely a perceptive person must actually sense her anguish, so intense was it. She swallowed painfully before managing to retort, 'And you will? Then I think you'd better pay just a little heed to the truth about Kemp Irvine, the real truth and not your idealistic imaginings, or you're going to be badly hurt.'

'And why should that concern you?' Emma retorted. 'What do you care what pain other people suffer?'

When her own was so all-enveloping? But what did Emma mean? Behind the sunglasses, Valentine's eyes searched the other girl's face, but at that moment Mrs Ducaine joined them and by unspoken agreement the hostilities were suspended. Mrs Ducaine was pleasant enough, although she produced a few oblique warnings to the effect that Valentine ought to tread warily now that her employer was on the spot and able to see how she was behaving, but Emma remained silent until they were joined by Kemp and some of the men who had shared in his game.

As the younger men swooped on her, Valentine watched Emma scramble to her feet, eagerly hurrying to greet Kemp, catching at his arm and looking confidingly up into his face.

Making intelligent comments about the game, Valentine still heard the other girl's anxious words. 'Oh, Kemp, Valentine has been saying you're not content to be at Fleurmont ... You're not going to go away again, are you?' she begged for reassurance most appealingly.

Kemp's smile was indulgent. 'We start harvesting at the end of next week, Emma, and I'll certainly be permanently at Fleurmont while that's going on.'

Then he looked in Valentine's direction with a definite hardening of his features, and his blue gaze was mocking. She experienced a moment of searing misery, but managed to give him a small, private smile which seemed to suggest that she knew his answer had merely been meant to appease Emma.

With a last contemptuous look, he gave his attention to Emma once more, and Valentine was left trying to subdue her poignant unhappiness while she pretended an interest in what the other men were saying to her.

Later, when Adam explained that he had to return to Fleurmont with Kemp and Valentine to pick up his car, Emma elected to accompany them. She clearly had her sights set on the front passenger seat as they approached the Porsche, and Valentine's unhappiness made her take perverse pleasure in suggesting that since Adam was so interested in the new car he ought to sit beside Kemp, as he had been in the back for their earlier journey. That, she thought complacently, was more subtle than claiming it for herself. But why was she bothering? She could achieve nothing for herself. Philip, Philip ... always his relationship to Kemp was in her mind.

Kemp gave her a malicious look and said smoothly, 'Adam, I can hardly believe it. Would you really pass up the opportunity to sit next to our ravishing Valentine?'

Adam looked at the gleaming car and then at the slim beauty that was Valentine.

'Valentine wins,' he said.

Her bright lips shaped a word and Kemp laughed quietly.

'Victory, Valentine,' he murmured. 'Over a machine.'

'I should hope so,' she retorted smartly, and treated Adam to a radiant smile.

At Fleurmont the brother and sister stayed for a drink, which they had in the pastel-coloured, scented garden with the evening sound of birdsong to punctuate their conversation.

'Don't forget you promised my mother you'd come over for lunch tomorrow, Kemp,' Emma reminded him when they left.

'What about you, Valentine?' Adam asked, squeezing her hand. 'Will you be over too?'

'Oh, I'm so sorry, Adam,' she said easily. 'But Gary has arranged to come over and go riding with me.'

'Oh, are you still trying to learn to ride, Valentine?' Emma asked gauchely.

'I'm succeeding too,' Valentine responded with quiet dignity which called attention to the other girl's crudeness, and Emma flushed.

They drove away and Kemp and Valentine turned towards the house. 'I hope you don't mind Gary using one of the horses,' she said quietly. 'Emma and Adam often ride them as well.'

'Of course I don't mind. They're all old friends and the horses need the exercise,' he assured her as they entered the beautiful hall. 'I'm glad to see you divide your favours equally, especially as neither Adam nor Gary means much to you.'

'Oh, I try to be fair,' she drawled nonchalantly, but his now familiar contempt still had the power to make her heart contract with hurt. Her sapphire eyes widened. 'Although I'm not sure what you mean by . . . my favours. The pleasure of my company, I suppose?'

'If that's all you give them,' Kemp said sceptically.

'It is.'

She looked at him expectantly then, to see if he believed her, but he merely raised his eyebrows derogatively.

'Why did you try to upset Emma?' he asked abruptly.

Valentine shook her head. 'She's going to be hurt, Kemp,' she warned. What would he say if she admitted that she too was going to be hurt; was already hurting badly?

'Let me handle it in my own way,' he snapped. 'Leave her alone in future, and I'd be grateful if you didn't discuss me with anyone else either.'

'All right,' she agreed equably. 'I don't like being talked about either.'

'You, Valentine?' He laughed at that. 'You'll be talked about all your life, sweetheart, and you know it. You'll also cause trouble all your life.'

It was too close to what Valentine knew of herself and for a fleeting moment the mask slipped fractionally, leaving her looking back at him helplessly. Then she managed a smile, but she couldn't make it anything other than bitter.

'You're probably right,' she conceded tartly.

By the time Valentine had enjoyed a scented bath and dressed for the evening, she had succeeded in subduing the pain that was part of her awareness of the appalling truth.

Her eyes were sparkling as she made up in front of her dressing-table mirror and she knew that she would enjoy this evening—it might be the last time she knew pleasure on Fleurmont, because when James and Sylvie left, she must tell Kemp the truth.

Her dress was another romantic dream, deep rose pink chiffon over masses of taffeta and net, unusual in that it had a very full skirt which swayed about her when she walked and emphasised the wonderful slenderness of her waist. The tight bodice revealed the firm perfection of her breasts and the heart-shaped neckline gave a tantalising glimpse of her cleavage. She had changed the colour of her lipstick, blusher and nail varnish, and softened her hairstyle, allowing a few shining curls to frame her face.

'The ultimate in femininity—not being ready at the stated time,' Kemp drawled when she finally joined him and the Hattinghs in the sitting-room. 'The ultimate in femininity anyway.'

'Oh, well!' Valentine was demurely apologetic even as she wondered achingly if he would ever address her without that contemptuous mockery. 'At least it allowed me to—Make An Entrance.'

'And what an entrance!' His eyes met hers which were like great sparkling jewels, and something passed between them, an exchange of something which left Valentine inwardly shaken and rejoicing in the knowledge that he found her desirable.

'Well worth waiting for,' James commented appreciatively.

'You always look so gorgeous, Valentine. Ah, if I was tall and dark,' Sylvie added ruefully, shaking her head. She was silvery fair and slight, in perfect contrast to her large dark husband.

'But I think you're lovely,' Valentine said, and meant it, as she sat down beside her. 'Who's looking after Binnie tonight?'

The evening passed enjoyably. Valentine was at her breathtaking best, and Salome had provided a delightful meal at a beautifully set table, while Kemp was a fascinating and attentive host.

Sipping at the estate's Cabernet Sauvignon, Valentine listened to the men discussing a new wine which had been created, the paradoxical Blanc de Noir. However much Kemp hated being burdened with Fleurmont, he clearly knew all there was to know about wine production.

James and Sylvie obviously liked and respected him, and once again Valentine felt that same sense of pride she had experienced at the polo. He was special, a rare and brilliant man with a magnetic power to attract.

But a facet of his attraction was physical, and as the evening progressed, she found herself stimulated as much by his physical presence as by his conversation, but in a wholly different way, for the effect was like a slow fire starting in her veins—and all so futile, her mind taunted inexorably.

It was late, midnight, when the Hattinghs departed. The night was dark and silent; the dogs had been fed and Salome and Maude had long since washed up and gone to their quarters, no doubt looking forward to sleeping late in the morning, Sunday being a day off for both of them.

Returning to the sitting-room with Kemp, Valentine was steeling herself to say what must be said.

She bent gracefully to test the heat of the last pot of coffee she had made, not so long ago. 'There's still some left if you'd like it,' she volunteered.

There was no reply and she turned to look at him questioningly. Kemp was standing in the centre of the room, simply looking at her, and his eyes were blazing in a quite unmistakable way. Valentine stood very still, staring back at him, but the rate of her heartbeats had accelerated.

The lights were dimmed to a low intimate glow and the room was very still, the only sound the ticking of the clock. Valentine felt as if she were suffocating, as if the room was too small to contain the intensity of feeling swamping her.

'Come here, Valentine,' Kemp invited softly.

For a moment longer she remained where she was, but her breath was coming sharp and shallow now. Then, with a sigh, she went to him.

This one last time, she promised herself weakly, and her awareness of the truth became torture.

She stood in front of him and his long sensitive fingers

lightly caressed the smooth line of her throat, causing a sensation that made her catch her breath.

'It's still only about twenty-four hours since I last held you in my arms,' Kemp murmured with a mockery that was for them both. 'You've been deliberately provocative all day, and tonight you look like a romantic fairytale princess—but fairytale creatures aren't for touching, are they, Valentine?'

'I don't think they ever feel as I do right now either,' she responded with a sad, faint smile, her voice a fine crystal sound.

He took her in his arms then and a shiver ran through her slender body as his lips touched her face, moving along one high cheekbone, then down until, in a sudden convulsive movement, their mouths fused. Instant, raging desire claimed Valentine and she clung to him, moving her arms up so that her trembling fingers could bury themselves in the clean thickness of the hair at the back of his head.

She moaned in supplication when the kiss came to an end and Kemp smiled at her, his face still very close to hers.

'There's too much skirt to that dress,' he said, a thread of laughter in his voice. 'I can't get close enough to you . . . And besides, I very much want to see what you look like.'

Valentine felt his fingers dealing with her zip, but she made no protest and allowed the rose pink confection to slide to the floor in a soft rustle of sound before stepping out of it. Then his arms claimed her again and they stood there, locked together in a timeless embrace, Valentine clad in her flimsy bra, the single taffeta half-slip which had not been attached to the dress and her high-heeled sandals.

She couldn't think, she could only feel. There was a drumming heartbeat sound which might have come from either of them and she felt she must surely die or at least faint as a result of this exquisite, throbbing pleasure.

Then Kemp was guiding her to the sofa, pushing her down and bending to remove her sandals, his hands warm on her slender, fine-boned feet.

'Although why the sofa I don't know, when there are several perfectly respectable beds in the house,' he murmured.

'Kiss me again,' she pleaded huskily, and he obliged while his fingers went to the fastening of her bra.

He was touching her tumescent breasts now, kneading the taut satin-textured flesh, and she gasped his name in desperate entreaty. She had never permitted lovemaking to go as far as this with any man, always being the one in control, and she was totally unprepared for the almost agonising delight of his touch.

Kemp raised himself to look down at her and drew a sharp breath. 'You're beautiful,' he said hoarsely, then put his mouth to the marble hardness of her nipples, and Valentine cried out, a long sobbing sound.

He lifted his head again after a time to see the intensity of passion that was transforming her face, leaving her eyes feverishly glittering while her parted lips were rosy and swollen, her head helplessly twisting and turning from side to side with her dark curls escaping the arrangement she had taken such trouble over earlier.

'What are you, Valentine?' he demanded with sudden harshness. 'All that passion, and how much feeling to go with it? As regal as a queen and as sensuous as a cat; Aphrodite's body hidden beneath a fairytale heroine's garments . . . Are you a purely carnal creature or do you experience emotion as well?

Desire was not enough; she knew that in some dazed recess of her mind, but still she drew him back to her, wanting to bind him to her for ever, till the end of all time. She must have unfastened the buttons of his white shirt because his chest was bare against her breasts and she was able to slide her hands over the heated dampness of his shoulders as his mouth found the moist sweetness of hers again.

She was like a wild creature in his arms, demented by her hunger and a growing hopelessness.

'You want this, don't you?' he groaned.

But she wanted more than his merely wanting her. She wanted a sharing of emotion—and truth. To allow him to take her not knowing what she had been in the life and death of his cousin would be despicable, because he would hate both her and himself when he found out.

'It's too soon,' she murmured with a break in her voice, striving to restrain that madness of desire which invited her to let this tempestuous lovemaking proceed to its natural conclusion.

'Too soon?' Sudden derision lightened his blue eyes as he levered himself away from her. 'Why be coy at this late date, sweetheart? It doesn't suit you. You know you're divine, a goddess created for love ... How many men have you allowed to make use of that exquisite body? How many have lost themselves in all that beauty and passion?'

He ran an insolent hand over her from throat to waist, and she shuddered, but managed to say stonily, 'None, Kemp.'

'None?' With a faint laugh he sat up and regarded her contemplatively. 'Truly, none?'

'Truly,' she said clearly.

She lay there, strangely unable to move. Her limbs felt heavy and an alien lethargy pervaded her being, making her eyes slumbrous as she looked back at him. She couldn't tell if he believed her or not and, at that at that moment, she didn't care. Nothing seemed to matter. She could even, in that soulless moment, have brought herself to tell him about Philip, but that didn't seem to matter either.

Kemp stood up and looked down at her, a searingly possessive look. Valentine lay where she was, heedless of the fact that her half-slip was ruched up around her thighs and she was uncovered from the waist up. Arms flung out, head tipped back on the slender white neck, dark hair brought to gypsy disorder by what had passed, she gazed back at him from beneath half-closed lids.

A faint smile came to his face. 'My God, do you know what you look like, lying there? Wild and wanton—you're nothing but an animal at this moment. If I touched you again you wouldn't give me another spiel about its being too soon.'

'And are you going to?' she asked with slow languor.

'It's my decision really, isn't it?' he queried grimly. 'No, Valentine, I'm not. You're probably right about its being too soon—how long have we known each other? But old habits die hard, I suppose . . . You see, in the course of my work I've been accustomed to doing without women for long periods since I couldn't take a woman to some of the places I had to go to. That's why, when a project came to an end, I'd remedy the situation at the earliest possible moment, knowing the next stretch of enforced celibacy wasn't far away. But here . . . We've all the time in the world, haven't we? I'll have to get used to that idea.'

'You're really a rather civilised man, aren't you?' she ventured, lips curving.

'I hope you appreciate it,' he retorted. 'But you yourself aren't at all civilised, are you, sweetheart? In my arms just now you were the complete savage, all sensation and nothing else, with your heart beating like any pagan drum under my hand.'

'I'm surprised at myself, I'll admit,' she confessed carefully as pain began to claim her again.

'You've never felt like that before?' he prompted.

'Never.'

'And I'll really be the first?'

'Yes,' she said simply. Only he wouldn't want her when he knew the truth about her. Ah, God, she could die of this terrible, tearing regret.

He looked at her strangely. 'Just as long as you do understand, Valentine, that it will be me . . . That we will be lovers eventually. It would be stupid to deny the physical attraction that exists between us, and ultimately it must be consummated. You do understand?'

'I've been waiting for you,' she said gravely, and her eyes, meeting his, were deep and tender with a promise because in that moment she was conscious only of the rightness of an eventual union between them. All that would finally keep them apart was forgotten again.

'Yes,' he said on an odd thoughtful note, and turned from her. 'Goodnight, Valentine. If I remain here any longer with the sight of you to tempt me, I'll forget that time is no longer of any importance.'

It was only some time later, after she had gone to bed, that sanity returned in full and painful measure.

Why, why hadn't she told him? To keep from doing so was merely inviting disaster as well as being unfair to them both.

And yet still she was tempted to delay her confession although she had the intelligence to realise that it was something she owed to herself as much as to Kemp.

He desired her and Valentine gloried in the knowledge, rejoicing in the fact that she had withheld her body from the countless other men who had desired it; had kept it for this one man whose passion could summon an answering fire in her blood.

But when she told him the truth he would no longer want her. For a moment she wished she had let him possess her fully, but in the next moment she knew that to have done so would have ultimately destroyed her—because it wasn't enough that Kemp should desire her sexually. She was greedy for more, so very much more, because she herself was driven by more than just the hunger of her body.

But love, or even liking, would take time to achieve, thanks to the brittle shell of sophistication she had hidden behind for so long. Underneath somewhere was the woman Kemp might have understood, the old Valli rather than Valentine, but to him Valli would be anathema.

'And I don't have time,' she whispered into the darkness, mocking the wild yearning that tempted her to withhold the truth from him still longer.

In the end, being human, she compromised, although she felt ashamed of the weakness that caused her to do so. She would allow herself time to win from him just one moment of genuine liking; a smile untinged with derision would suffice, or amusement without mockery.

Just that, no more, and it would have to last her all her life because then she must tell him. But she would have to be quick about it because the truth must be told, for both their sakes.

She had little contact with Kemp the following day, since Sunday was a day on which she often slept late, and he departed for the Ducaine estate in the middle of the morning. Soon after he had gone, Gary arrived, and Valentine prepared a light lunch which they ate outside before riding two of the horses into the foothills.

It was a lazy day, as Sundays ought to be, and it wasn't too difficult to divert Gary when he showed signs of wanting to take their relationship a step further.

Valentine told herself she was using the time to relax and gather strength for what she had to do, but her mind was constantly active yet bringing her no closer to a solution.

It was late afternoon when they got back and handed the horses over to Freddie Jansen.

'A drink before you go, Gary?' Valentine suggested hospitably, and he accepted eagerly.

There was no sign of the Porsche, so Kemp must still be over at the Ducaine estate. Sipping her gin and tonic, Valentine wondered just what he felt for Emma. The other girl could never satisfy him . . .

He belongs to me, I belong to him—it was the first time she had formed the thought with such clarity, and a secretive little smile tugged at her lips and disappeared in another moment when the weight of reality came dropping down on her like an avalanche: there was still a truth in her life called Philip de Villiers. There could be no altering of the past.

'When will I see you again?' Gary demanded a little later when she had skilfully implanted in his mind the idea that he ought to be leaving.

'Ring me some time during the week,' Valentine advised lightly.

They stood in the driveway beside which his car was parked, under one of the huge oaks, and he shook his flaxen head in reluctant admiration.

'You never give an inch, do you?'

She smiled. 'If I did, you'd take the proverbial mile.'

'I'll take a kiss to be going on with.'

She didn't mind. However many men kissed her, the memory of Kemp's possession of her mouth could never be overlaid.

Gary held her tightly, but she felt nothing, and his greedy kiss ignited no spark of longing. The whisper of tyres came to her ears and she disengaged herself, smiling slightly at the sight of the silver Porsche. Even a moment of jealousy from Kemp would satisfy her, she thought with wistful yearning.

'Valentine!' Gary thought the smile was for him.

'Goodbye, Gary,' Valentine said gently, and forgot him.

CHAPTER FOUR

KEMP was waiting for her outside the house when Valentine returned after Gary had driven away. She approached him unselfconsciously, her bright lips curving. She might not yet be a skilled horsewoman, but she knew how well riding clothes suited her tall slim figure. Her breeches fitted like another skin and were tucked into beautifully polished boots, and her cream silk shirt had the sleeves rolled up and several buttons seductively open to expose her tender throat and just a suggestion of the hollow between her breasts.

A twisted ironic smile greeted her. 'Adam will be insanely jealous. When does he get his share?'

Valentine tilted her head to one side, regarding him curiously. 'I'm deeply disappointed,' she mocked liltingly and with what truth only she knew, suffering like the damned and never revealing a fraction of it. 'You're the one supposed to be insanely jealous.'

'You must have forgotten what you told me last night; that I'm the only man who can arouse you to that extent,' he reminded her tauntingly. 'I'm merely interested. What do you get in exchange for the kisses and whatever else you allow your devoted swains?'

Valentine lifted a graceful shoulder. 'Nothing. I'm just of a naturally obliging nature.'

'Like all tarts.'

'Well, it is generosity that makes tarts of certain women,' she retorted, unabashed.

'And you're very generous, aren't you?' Kemp's eyes held hers, challenging her.

A slow, ravishing smile made her beauty something rare and elevated, almost unearthly, but she felt she must faint with the effort. She yearned to fling herself at him, begging him to understand, to forgive, but she knew she would be rejected.

'I could be.'

'My God, I feel sorry for any man who can't see through your act,' he said disgustedly, turning from her to enter the house. 'Enjoy yourself while you can, Valentine—or allow Adam and Gary to do so . . . Because the flirtation game ends when we become lovers, my beautiful bitch.'

But they would not become lovers, and Valentine knew it with a fresh chill. There was Philip, always Philip . . .

One morning the following week, during a lull between visitors, she glanced idly at the calendar on which she had taken to writing her estimate of the daily number of visitors over each day's date. A moment later her eyes began to sparkle and she picked up the telephone receiver. The gathering of the grapes would get under way any day now, but first—

'Sylvie?' Valentine queried. 'Could you take over from me for a short while up here? I find I have to go to Stellenbosch.'

'Of course,' Sylvie was eager to oblige. 'Make it longer than a short while if you'd rather go to Cape Town.'

'Stellenbosch will do.'

But some time later, when Valentine had driven in to the beautiful university town with its backdrop of blue mountains, famous Stellenryck Wijn Museum and beautiful historic buildings, she encountered some difficulty in finding just what she wanted until she entered a tiny stationery shop she had never come across before.

'You took some time off today?' Kemp mentioned enquiringly at dinner that evening.

'Yes, is that all right?' she asked with a hint of mischief in her eyes, knowing too agonisingly well that this might be the last opportunity she had to appear appealing in his eyes and thus defiantly intent on making her last performance a flawless one. 'You see, my hours of duty coincide with shopping hours.'

'As long as Sylvie doesn't mind,' he said easily. 'What are you looking so pleased about?'

'Was I?' The smile she cast him was wholly engaging and she was devastated to see his expression harden in response. Ah, dear God, was she to have no happy memory of a pleasant exchange with him? 'Well, I am feeling pleased.'

Kemp watched her for a moment, noting that her lovely, delicate face was more expressively mobile than usual. She sat opposite him, fingering the stem of her glass with scarlet-tipped fingers, consciously alluring in her frivolous navy blue organza, deliberately enchanting.

'Why?' A slight smile touched his mouth.

A gurgle of laughter, sheer seduction, escaped her, and it had a ring of genuine amusement, for despite her sadness over what must come, she was feeling excited. 'I can't tell you now, but you will find out, I promise you.'

'You're up to something,' he guessed, eyes narrowed as he surveyed her. 'I don't trust you at all, Valentine. You're a very dangerous lady.'

'No, relax, please!' she insisted demurely, playing to the hilt. Her swan song, she thought anguishedly behind the mask; after tomorrow came the real pain, the real loneliness. 'It's nothing wicked or bad. It's simply a wonderful idea I had this morning.'

'Your ideas are all likely to be wicked, sweetheart.'

'You just don't know me, Kemp,' she protested gently.

'I know all I need to,' he assured her sharply.

'Don't you wish you understood me?' she challenged.

'Oh, I understand you, Valentine,' he said meaningfully, and she thought his voice contained a threat. 'I understand you only too well, which is why I don't wish to know any more.'

'Now you're getting too clever for me,' she withdrew from the conversation with a smile. 'But I'm going to surprise you one day, Kemp . . . tomorrow, in fact!'

He didn't take her seriously and the subject was changed, but when they parted later Valentine was still smiling.

Kemp had not touched her again that week, although he had had plenty of opportunity to do so, especially as they were alone together in the evenings. Occasionally, testing his control, or perhaps her power, Valentine had been deliberately enticing—or perhaps she simply wanted to experience his lovemaking again. But the more blatantly seductive she was, the greater grew the derision with which he habitually regarded her. She had to be a masochist, she thought disgustedly. Joy would never be her lot in life.

Yet, in a strange, perverse way, she enjoyed the challenge, almost a contest between them, and wished it might continue until she had made him see her as she really was, but that would take too long. Soon now, the real agony must begin. But could it be any worse than this present pain, half guilt and half regret?

The next morning she dressed herself in a scarlet dress with off-the-shoulder sleeves and a deep frill round the low neck, a flounce edging the skirt and a matching belt clasped about her slender waist, knowing that, being tall, she could carry off the feminine frills and flounces she loved. She wore her hair in a smooth style that day, and the silver studs in her ears were her only jewellery.

She waited until she knew Kemp was in the breakfast room before going along, her high-heeled red sandals tapping out an unhasty, measured rhythm. In her hand she held a medium sized envelope.

'Good morning.' Her smile was brilliant, masking both nervousness and excitement as she held out the envelope with his first name written on it in her elaborate handwriting. 'This is for you.'

'What's this? Formal notice?' he enquired mildly.

'Oh, no. Think of today's date,' she suggested as she sat down.

'The fourteenth of February?' Kemp opened the envelope.

The card she had finally chosen lacked the crude garishness of so many modern ones, since the designer had nostalgically reverted to an older style, but Valentine had crossed out the verse it contained and written simply, I'll be your Valentine.

Kemp sat back in his chair, his eyes glinting. 'A clear invitation if ever there was one. They're supposed to be anonymous, though.' He read her inscription again and began to laugh. 'But you are already, aren't you?'

The tragic irony of the situation engulfed her, but she forced her red lips into a smile. 'Yes,' she admitted, and pleasure touched her pain because she had made him laugh. The feeling was swiftly followed by the most profound sadness she had ever experienced as she remembered what must come soon—today. She went on, 'I have surprised you, haven't I? I said I would.'

'Oh, you're a very clever and original woman,' he conceded indulgently, still smiling. 'You'll never be predictable, will you?'

Her long eyelashes fluttered. Just a little longer, she thought, and knew she was being self-indulgent. 'Although I'm not sure it was wise. I've just this minute recalled the terrible effect of a Valentine on Boldwood in Hardy's *Far From the Madding Crowd*!'

'I remember how marvellously the late Peter Finch did that scene in the film, sitting there with the clock ticking away, just staring at it,' Kemp laughed.

'Brooding, slowly going out of his mind,' Valentine supplemented with wicked relish.

'No, sweetheart, you'll never drive me out of my mind,' he said warningly.

'I wouldn't want to,' she retorted with a faint shudder, remembering Philip and feeling her pleasure diminishing. Perhaps she would be the one to go out of her mind.

Kemp gave her another smile. 'Would today by any chance be a special occasion for you?'

'Twenty-two today,' she said with a slight lilt.

'Happy birthday, then,' he congratulated her, getting up and coming round the table to her. 'I've nothing to give you, but——'

'Yes, you have,' she interrupted provocatively. Just this one last time she would not deny herself. After today came the unloved, untouched loneliness cruel fate had chosen for her.

'Yes, I have,' he agreed, pulling her up out of her chair and turning her into his arms.

A soft sigh of surrender came from her as she felt his lips touch hers, his tongue flickering over their sensitivity while his hands caressed the exposed skin of her shoulders. Neither of them heard the entry and subsequent hasty departure of Salome Jansen who grinned to herself.

Valentine could scarcely credit the mingled tenderness and sensuality of Kemp's kiss as he invaded her mouth more fully. Their lips were entwined in wondrous communication, signalling their desire, and his hands moved gently all over her body, touching her back and breasts and midriff, hips and thighs, burning through the soft material of her dress, echoing the message of his mouth, and she felt the unmistakable swelling that told her how much he wanted her.

'Kemp!' She felt as if she was melting and there was a trembling weakness somewhere deep inside her.

'I can hardly believe in you,' he murmured, lifting his head to look into the passion-darkened sapphire eyes. 'You're incredible!'

'So are you,' she replied in a shaken voice.

'And mine—all mine?' he probed.

'All yours,' she confirmed, delivering her life to him with a smile that cost her more dearly than anything that had gone before.

Kemp held her away from him. 'I'll take you to dinner somewhere in Stellenbosch tonight, some place where we can dance. All right?'

'Yes.'

She couldn't mar the perfection of this moment, but she guessed that the outing would never taken place because by tonight he would know the truth about her. She knew he intended that the evening should culminate in the consummation of the attraction between them, but she must and would find the courage to tell him about Philip.

She turned away rather quickly as he released her, for once unable to trust her usually invincible composure, so poignant was the regret she felt for what she would be passing up.

'Your lipstick has disappeared,' Kemp laughed as he sat down again, but by then the mask was firmly back in place and Valentine was able to smile at him with eyes that brimmed with pure delight. God forgive her, but she couldn't say the words to lose him in this precious hour.

That morning was for treasuring the memory of their exchange in the breakfast room, reliving each moment of it with an absorption which made her over-generous with the wine she poured out for those visitors who had come to taste Fleurmont's product. It was also a time of sadness, but there was no doubt in Valentine's mind that when she saw Kemp at lunch she would make her confession.

She had won a moment of tenderness from him, and laughter. They must suffice. She now felt herself steeled to her duty by a strength of will she had not possessed before.

A pair of Frenchmen arriving late delayed her slightly, for she always felt she ought to take extra trouble and time with visitors from other wine-producing countries, and France was after all the most famous of them all.

She was smiling when she went to lunch because they had been appreciative, not at all condescending, genuine wine-lovers and far less affected than some of the pompous would-be connoisseurs with whom she had dealings.

Freddie Jansen had just got back from collecting the Fleurmont mail when Valentine joined Kemp at the table in the garden, and he gave them both an interested look before departing.

Kemp raised his eyebrows in amused enquiry and Valentine shrugged.

'Well, we know all about grapevines in this part of the world,' she laughed.

'We do indeed. Yours.' Kemp had finished sorting through the mail and handed her four white envelopes. 'Birthday cards or Valentines?'

'Well, this is from home—my parents,' she said, examining the postmarks and handwriting. 'And this, from Newcastle in Natal, will be from my brother Nigel. He's a chemical engineer.'

She sat down and poured herself a glass of Clairette Blanche. She opened Nigel's card first because she loved her brother very much, then dealt with the others while Kemp was opening a large envelope with the address typed on to it. The two unsigned Valentines, since they were posted in Stellenbosch, she attributed to Adam and Gary.

'Valli . . .'

She looked up at that, every vestige of colour draining from her face, and met the bitter contempt in Kemp's blue eyes.

'Valli McLaren,' he repeated softly, dangerously.

'I was going to tell you,' she gulped. 'But how . . .?'

The corners of his mouth turned down in a grimace of the utmost distaste as he handed her several old newspaper cuttings, some of them with photographs.

'Oh, God,' she said hollowly. Then seeing the terrible anger in his face she sought to defend herself with the flippancy that had so frequently proved one of her most effective weapons. 'Is there going to be another Valentine's Day Massacre, Kemp?'

'Why didn't you tell me?' he rapped, taking the cuttings back.

'I was going to.' She was trembling violently, unable to find any sort of control.

'Oh, I believe you,' he retorted sarcastically. 'When? After you'd seen how much damage you could inflict?'

'Today! Now . . . at lunch!' she said desperately.

'Don't lie to me, Valentine . . . Valli! Was that what Philip called you? God, if only Edward had used your name when he wrote to me about what had happened—but he called you by a title I've no doubt you deserve. If you'd meant to tell me, you'd have done so before now—at our very first meeting.'

Valentine stared at the bunch of cuttings he still held in his hand, those terrible pieces penned for the entertainment of the readers of scandal sheets, with information supplied to the writers by so-called friends. The destruction of her privacy, the distortions to her life and personality had inflicted a wound that would never fully heal. She had felt raw and naked for months afterwards, flinching at recognition, hurt deep into her soul by the knowledge that there were people who would believe the things that had been said and written about her, because everything there was based on truth, although grotesquely manipulated to give a different impression.

She flung her head up in a sudden gesture of pride. 'I only made the connection after coming home from that party—when I saw Philip's photo in the main bedroom,' she said with quiet intensity. 'Believe me, Kemp.'

But it was as if he were looking at a stranger, his eyes blank, devoid of recognition. He glanced down at the pieces of newspaper in his hand and read some of the captions, ineffably disgusted by the clichés.

'Lady Havoc—The Queen of Hearts—De Villiers Not Valli's First Disaster . . . what does that mean?'

'Oh, you might as well know the worst of me,' she flung at him bitterly, her mouth in tragic downturned contrast to its usual smiling shape. 'I attract disaster like a magnet, Kemp. I've got the opposite of the Midas touch in emotional matters . . . Everyone who comes into contact with me suffers for it. I'm dangerous, do you understand? When I was seventeen I went out with a boy who was doing his military service ... He wanted a more serious relationship, but I wasn't in love with him. He was ... oh, hell! Do I have to repeat all this? He was desperately unhappy and he volunteered for border duty ... He was killed in a landmine explosion. Some of my ... good, loyal friends remembered that and told those ... those hacks! They also remembered other men ... Philip was the final victim of my curse. Now you know.'

'Yes! Philip ... my cousin!' Kemp looked at another report with a fairly large and clear photograph accompanying it.

Valentine shuddered. That was one of the most painful memories. 'You drove him to death, you killed him ... murdered him!' Reinette de Villiers had screamed that day after the inquest was over, and the black and white photograph showed her with her mouth a gaping wound as she gave vent to her anguished hatred while her husband attempted to hustle her away and Valentine, a straight, erect and isolated figure, seemed to wear an expression of cold hauteur which had, in fact, been a shield against the lacerating humiliation and shame of that moment, proudly refusing to hide her face from the camera men.

She saw Kemp's fist clench, the knuckles whitening as he crushed the various pieces of yellowing paper into a ball, and, raising her eyes, she saw that the tanned skin was stretched tautly over the bones of his face.

'You bitch,' he condemned her quietly.

'What would you have me do?' she asked with coldly bitter pride. 'Take a razor to my looks, be less than myself, to prevent men I can't love falling in love with me and then being unable to handle their rejection?'

Her head was high and her sapphire eyes flashed with resentment.

'Your relationship with Philip had been going on for some time,' Kemp reminded her harshly. 'If you knew you could never feel anything for him, why the hell did you go on seeing him? And didn't the existence of a wife concern you?'

'I didn't know he was married,' Valentine flared. Then, gaining a measure of control, she went on haughtily, 'But I don't have to defend myself to you or anyone else. I know the truth and that's all that counts. The rest of you can believe what you like.'

'It was that same self-centredness that made you continue seeing Philip, wasn't it?' he accused her. 'You didn't think of him, you didn't care about anyone's feelings save your own.'

She drew a steadying breath and explained icily, 'I went on seeing Philip because I was stupid enough to judge other men by my brother. I now realise that was a terrible insult to Nigel ... He's rational and well-balanced. He doesn't expect every girl he goes out with to feel love or lust; he's been content with simply getting on well with them, enjoying the company of girls who share his interests ... Philip and I had many mutual tastes. I was very, very foolish, I know, but lest your opinion of me isn't low enough already, Kemp, let me add that I never shed one single tear over your cousin. His final act was one of childish and spiteful cowardice. I resent him— I hate and despise him for what he did to me.'

'How typically selfish! All you can think of is what was done to you.' Kemp's expression was unyielding. 'I'm not interested in hearing any more of your explanations and excuses. Get out of my sight, Valentine ... I've seen enough violence in the world to loathe it in every form but, my God, I can understand violence today.'

Valentine stood up swiftly. 'First, though——' She stretched an arm over the table and snatched the crumpled cuttings from him. 'Who would do this? Who made it their responsibility to inform you of the truth in this sordid manner?'

'I wondered if you knew?'

'It would be nobody I know. I severed all my relationships after ... after Philip's death. Too many of my

so-called friends had proved too eager to jump into the
act of making sure all Cape Town knew just how callous
the notorious Valli McLaren could be. None of them
knows where I am or . ... that you're my employer.' Her
mouth drooped bitterly as she smoothed the pieces of
paper. She turned one over and her eyes hardened. 'My
God, look at this! They've been glued into a scrapbook at
some stage. What sort of mind do you need to make such
a collection?'

'Sordid, I'll agree, but all you deserve, Valentine,'
Kemp said bitingly.

She picked up the envelope in which the cuttings had
arrived. The date was smudged, but—'Cape Town.' Her
eyes narrowed as she thought for a moment, then she met
his gaze levelly. 'Yet I could swear this was done by
someone from around here, Kemp.'

'Possibly.' He shrugged. 'But you'll make no accusations. You've no right to justice, Valentine. Now go . . .
and take those with you. I don't want to see them.'

'Am I fired?' She was defiant.

'Yes!' Kemp said explosively. 'Go, Valentine.'

'My contract states a month's notice from either side,'
she taunted, and went, intent only on finding a box of
matches so that she could burn these pieces of paper. Even
her hand felt defiled, just holding them.

She passed Freddie Jansen without seeing him, her
head held high and her red mouth tight. He looked after
her concernedly before going in search of his wife.

'You see, our soil is red and deep,' Valentine explained
to the man who had said he was a maize farmer from the
Transvaal. She heard someone enter the room, but she
kept her eyes fastened on the man's open, friendly face,
her smile unwavering. 'But additionally, we get a sea-
breeze over the estate in the afternoons—you wouldn't
think we'd benefit at this distance, would you?—and that
breeze is the reason for the excellence of our red wines.'

'Thank you for explaining, Miss,' he said cheerfully.

'Wine-production always seemed to me to have a certain mystique, but it's not so different to any other sort of farming, is it?'

'Soil and climate are the great dictators here as well,' Valentine said. 'Now, have you decided what you'd like in your triple pack?'

She dealt with the sale pleasantly, ignoring the presence of Kemp, for it was he who had entered, accompanied by the dogs.

Not by a look or a gesture did she betray that inwardly she was almost in a state of collapse. The afternoon had been hellish; every moment had been emotional torture and dealing as charmingly as ever with the public had required every last vestige of her considerable acting ability.

But now the last visitor of the day was taking his leave, thanking her profusely. It was too late to expect any more, Maude had already removed the glasses the man had used for tasting and, but for Kemp's unexpected presence, Valentine would have collapsed wearily into her chair.

Instead, she turned to face him with a cool little smile. 'I expect you're wondering what I'm doing, still here. I did remind you of the clause stating one month's notice was required, I believe?'

The remoteness of his expression chilled her. 'That's what I came to tell you—I've changed my mind about that, Valentine. I'm keeping you here.'

Valentine was immobile. 'Why?'

'Have you forgotten my once telling you what I'd like to do to the woman who destroyed Philip?' he enquired silkily. 'I said I'd take her and break her, Valentine . . . I'll see you at my feet before I let you go, sweetheart. You told me earlier, and with what pride, that you had never wept for my cousin. I'll make you weep to rival the Cape winter rains.'

'In that case, I'm the one giving notice,' she said tartly.

'You'll stay,' Kemp stated inexorably.

'Vengeance doesn't become you, Kemp.'

'Nevertheless . . .' He shrugged dismissively and she shuddered inwardly at the menace of his tone.

'And to think I once said you were civilised!' she lashed.

'Only civilised women merit civilised treatment . . . Valli!' He uttered the terrible name with such appalling hatred that she took an involuntary step backwards without realising it.

She wondered how much more she could endure. Pain was exploding within her, agonising, sparking pain, and the hatred she felt against fate was so intense that it frightened her. Was she never to know peace in her life? Chet was close beside her, his Great Dane's face quizzical, and she dropped a hand to his head. She felt faint, the result of a surfeit of emotion, plus the fact that she had gone without lunch.

Then she lifted her head in a curious gesture of acceptance, as if signalling her readiness to endure whatever Kemp might choose to do to her, and in that moment she became strong again.

'May I go?' she asked quietly.

He inclined his head slightly. 'Don't forget we have a dinner date. Be ready to leave at seven.'

'I would have thought that was off,' she ventured as she walked to the door.

'Why?' He spoke harshly. 'You're a woman any man would be proud to be seen with—just as long as no one guessed what lay beneath that breathtaking beauty. Wear one of your most dazzling confections, Valli, something ravishing enough to make every man in the place desire you.'

She paused, looking back over her shoulder. 'You can't humiliate me that way, Kemp.'

'No?' The threat was blatant, and she felt as if he had become a stranger. 'By the time I've finished with you, there won't be a shred of that glorious pride left; I want you humble to the point of humiliation.'

'This is unworthy of you,' she said icily, and walked out.

Later she took perverse pleasure in obeying Kemp's injunction regarding her appearance. The black georgette dress was simpler than most that she owned, yet infinitely more seductive for it was cut very low, with shoe-string straps supporting it at the shoulders, and it was fitted to reveal every curve and contour from the waist up, while the skirt hung in fine soft folds to her knees. With it she wore seamed black silk stockings, one of her most luxurious extravagances, and flimsy high-heeled black sandals. It was somehow a decadent outfit, she thought, smiling acidly to herself in the mirror, and her silver jewellery suited it, as did the exotic make-up which she applied lavishly, feeling the need of a mask. Even Kemp, hating her as he now did, was going to catch his breath . . .

His eyes narrowed when she walked into the hall where he was waiting for her.

'Quite stunning, Valentine,' he congratulated her sardonically. 'Especially that make-up—somehow maquillage seems a more appropriate word. No wonder my poor cousin lost his head as well as his heart! Most men would, knowing nothing of the truth that lies beneath the beauty, because not only are you very lovely; you also have great charm and the ability to entertain and amuse.'

That tragic mouth he had once seen when he had caught her in a defenceless moment was in evidence again for a second.

'Yes. It did once seem as if all those things were gifts with which I'd been blessed.' She paused and forced a brittle self-mocking smile. 'In the end, though, they turned out to be a curse.'

'For the men they attracted,' Kemp qualified harshly.

'Oh, God! Do you really think I haven't suffered too?' she asked quietly. 'Only a stupid person could fail to do so, and I'm by no means stupid, Kemp.'

'True. You're too clever to be trusted,' he drawled.

She looked at him with a strange dignity in her great sapphire eyes, even while part of her was reacting to the mere sight and physical presence of him, tall and devastatingly attractive in his evening clothes. Then she turned gracefully to precede him out of the house, knowing too well that this would be the pattern of the evening that lay ahead of them, with every word Kemp uttered calculated to wound. She had only her inherent belief in her own worth as a protection.

In fact, the evening turned into a nightmare. The restaurant at which Kemp had reserved a table was one of the most luxurious in Stellenbosch: the décor was tasteful but wildly expensive, the lighting subtle, the music romantic but unobtrusive, and there was a choice of delicious Cape-Dutch and French dishes, while the wine-list boasted only the most respected of estate wines. The clientele, too, fitted their surroundings: no students were to be found here. Some of the people at the tables or on the small dance-floor were middle-aged, while the younger ones had an affluent sleekness, that self-assured absence of tension that made them look as if they had stepped out of one of the Peter Stuyvesant films.

With her head held high, Valentine felt rather than saw the eyes that swivelled in their direction as they entered and a waiter greeted them in hushed tones and took them to their table. It was as it had been at the polo club, the attention they were attracting, yet different somehow, because now she felt none of the pride she had felt then. She felt exposed: the men's looks were an invasion of her privacy, and Kemp, though he had a hand at her back, afforded her no protection. This was the way he wanted it, she knew. He wanted to humiliate her.

She looked at him across the beautifully appointed table with its fresh flowers and exquisite linen, the silver winking and the crystal sparkling in the light of the tall pink candles. His face was harder than she had ever seen it and her heart became like a stone in her breast. There was only one thing she could do, and that was to endure.

Kemp ordered champagne. 'Happy birthday, Valentine,' he toasted her ironically.

'I trust you're deriving some enjoyment from this

farce,' she retorted frostily. 'I'm afraid I'm not.'

'We'll dance when we've eaten. You'll feel better then,' he drawled.

The torture went on, and on. Normally Valentine would have derived great pleasure from such an outing and the elegant surroundings, but tonight she was oblivious of everything save the hard, unrelenting face of the man opposite her. She could expect no mercy from him. She barely knew what she ate as she sat there, doing her best to appear unconcerned when every remark he addressed to her was a contemptuous taunt.

'You won't break me this way, Kemp,' she warned him once, picking up her glass and sipping composedly.

'And yet I'll break you, Valentine,' he promised with such savage conviction that she felt sick.

His blue eyes burned bright and hard as they traversed her expressionless face before travelling over the pearly whiteness of her neck to where the low-cut gown revealed the soft swell of her breasts. His glance seemed to caress her, but with an insolence that was shocking.

Valentine felt as if he had actually touched her and her stomach churned, the muscles contracting painfully even as she forced herself to stare coolly back at him when his eyes claimed hers again.

When he led her on to the dance-floor the nightmare intensified. The way he held her, caught fast against the hard length of his body, was devoid of any consideration for her feelings or physical comfort. There was no tenderness or respect or even desire, only a wish to hurt and humiliate. A glance at the unseeing brilliance of his eyes and the cruel curl of his lips confirmed this for Valentine, and she felt something die within her.

Kemp hauled her still closer, every movement of his body an insult, his hands and arms careless of the pain they were inflicting. Slow, creeping shame began to wash through Valentine, eventually flooding her entire being. Dear God, even like this, even being solely used by him, she could feel that hollow ache which only he could fill.

She wanted to grind her hips against him, and lift her arms and cling—Ah, God help her, was Kemp aware of it?

'Valli . . .' The name was a derisive taunt. He bent his head. His lips touched the side of her neck, searing the silken skin.

The sound of the music seemed to fade. All Valentine was conscious of was the heavy thunderous beat of her heart. They were barely moving now, and Kemp's hands at her back, one at her waist and the other higher up where her skin was bare, were shaping and controlling her, making of her whatever he willed her to be. The warmth of his body against hers was all heaven and hell, and her breathing was betraying her.

'I'm Valentine,' she insisted raggedly.

'Valli,' he mocked again, and her shame exploded.

She tipped her head back, forcing him to see the sapphire flash of her eyes in her tense white face. Her scarlet lips parted.

'You have the right to be angry with me, Kemp,' she said clearly. 'You have the right to hate me. But you do not have the right to treat me as a whore!'

CHAPTER FIVE

THE fine lines about Kemp's eyes seemed to have deepened and his smile was cruelly ironic as he heard her words.

'And you, my sweet Valentine, have no right to beg for mercy—when you showed none to my cousin,' he added softly.

'I would never beg for anything from you,' she retorted, keeping her voice low because there were other couples dancing close to them. 'I'm merely asking—requesting—that you see me as I am, and treat me accordingly.'

'And what are you?' His voice menaced her.

'Many bad things, I have no doubt,' she conceded bitterly. 'But I'm not your whore.'

'Whose, then?' The words flicked at wounds both old and new like the curling end of a whip. 'Philip's? Was he your lover?'

'No.'

'God, what a fool he must have been!' Kemp's laughter was mirthless. 'You used him and gave nothing in return.'

Valentine's chin lifted. 'Why the hell should I have?'

'Why the hell shouldn't you?'

'Because——' She drew a sharp breath. 'Because you're looking at the last of the great idealists, Kemp. I was the poor fool; I really believed it all, the lovely myth ... Some day my prince will come, or at the very least Mr Right. No, perhaps it wasn't that exactly. I just believed that one day I would recognise someone and until then ... Well, I was waiting. But I was young, and I thought that meant making friends, having fun. All my contemporaries were playing the dating game, so I did too, all through my varsity years and after. I'd just got my first job and a flat of my own in one of those old houses in Rondebosch when I met Philip——'

'I think we'll order more coffee and then leave,' Kemp interrupted abruptly, releasing her arm and propelling her towards their table.

'Didn't you stop to think what you were doing to Philip?' he asked over the coffee.

Valentine shook her head. She was so tense that her entire body ached and it was an effort to answer clearly, 'How could I? He was just someone I went out with.'

'You bitch!' he breathed, shaking his head. 'It really was as simple and undemanding as that, as far as you were concerned, wasn't it? That your effect on men was lethal just didn't concern you. Don't try to tell me you were unaware of your power as a very beautiful and engaging woman.'

'As it happens, I wasn't fully aware of it then,' she defended herself icily. 'That first boy, the one who volunteered for border duty ... Well, as I got a bit older, I thought it was his youth that had made him over-sensitive. But it's true that at varsity I was always disappointed when boy-friends overreacted to a break-up ... It took Philip to open my eyes. You needn't worry, Kemp: I finally and painfully learnt my lesson. No one else will suffer from my curse. I now avoid nice sensitive men like the plague ... I remember you couldn't understand, at our first meeting, why I should prefer Adam and company to Henry van Wyk. Well, I didn't, but Henry would suffer over me; the others wouldn't.'

'The great tragedy queen,' Kemp derided.

'You speak more truly than you realise,' she countered, and an arrogant tilt came to her head. 'It's as if I carry the doom of nice young men with me wherever I go ... Except that Philip proved not at all nice in the end. He didn't tell me he was married and I was stupid enough to assume that if a wife wasn't mentioned, then a wife didn't exist. These days I always ask.'

'You're really doing your best to convince me that you're more sinned against than sinning, aren't you?' he mocked.

Her mouth curved bitterly. 'It's a terrible thing, to be beautiful. Can you understand that? But I refuse to become a nun or to tone it down even a degree. I can quote Popeye: I yam wot I yam! It's others who must learn to bear it.'

'I daresay Helen took the same attitude all those years ago,' Kemp drawled. 'At least you haven't caused a war yet, Valentine.'

His eyes were cold, refusing to understand her, failing to recognise the burden which she carried but which she would never allow to crush her. To compromise would be to betray herself. Her avoidance of the nice young men like Henry van Wyk was as far as she would go.

'I'd like to leave,' she requested flatly.

The drive back to Fleurmont, through the velvety warmth of the February night, was accomplished in almost total silence.

On arrival, Valentine left the car the minute it stopped and went to the house, extracting her own key from the tiny black pochette she had carried. But once in the hall, she waited, listening to the sound of the garage being closed.

Then Kemp's voice was heard for a moment, pacifying the dogs, before he entered the hall and closed and locked the door behind him.

'Well?' he asked enquiringly as he looked at her still form and expressionless face.

A brittle smile came fleetingly. 'Am I supposed to thank you for this evening, Kemp?'

'Not if you didn't enjoy it,' he replied indifferently.

'You didn't intend that I should, did you?' she challenged bitterly.

'Perhaps it will console you to know that I didn't derive any enjoyment from it either.'

'I suppose I didn't suffer enough to satisfy your tastes,' she lashed.

'You evidently credit me with very sadistic tastes,' he drawled thoughtfully. 'You do agree that you deserve to suffer, sweetheart?'

'No. I don't think I deserve to, but I fully expect to,' she told him wearily, turning away. 'But I'd be grateful if you could postpone your vengeance until another day, Kemp. This has been a long and eventful day; I don't remember any of my other birthdays being this full of incident.'

'It's not over yet, either,' Kemp warned her quietly.

She walked down the passage to her bedroom, staring straight ahead of her, knowing he was following. At the door she put a hand out to switch on the bedroom light before finally facing him again.

'I'm not sleeping with you, if that's what you mean,' she stated coldly.

'No?'

His eyes rested briefly on her set face, noting the fragile bone-structure. Then they moved on, examining her pale shoulders and the curve of her breasts. In her turn, Valentine stared back at him, wondering resignedly how she should handle this and, at the same time, realising that she hadn't seen him look this tired since the night they had met, and then he had spent most of the day travelling. There were grooves bracketing that pain-twisted mouth and the lines about his eyes were more like deep cuts tonight.

Their eyes met again, clashing, and she recognised the burning expression in his.

'Well, what's it to be, Kemp?' she taunted maliciously. 'Are you going to rape me in revenge; take for yourself what I denied to Philip?'

'You and I together could never equal rape, my beautiful bitch,' he denied with a faint, humourless smile. 'But as for taking what was denied to Philip—well, why the hell not?'

He had a reckless, restless look about him as he advanced and Valentine felt a stirring of panic, realising the dangerousness of his mood.

'For God's sake, Kemp,' she murmured helplessly, but already he was dragging her against him, his lips finding the tantalising redness of hers.

He held her fast, in a grip of steel, so that her struggles were unavailing.

'I don't know you any more,' she protested when eventually the assault on her mouth ended. 'You're like a stranger.'

'I could say ditto, Valentine,' he countered harshly. 'I had thought I was beginning to know and understand you, right up until lunchtime today.'

Then his mouth came down on hers again, with bruising pressure. Valentine twisted and turned in his grasp, but it was no use, and she was weak with exhaustion when finally he picked her up and carried her the short distance to the bed, laying her down and flinging himself on to her, his lips immediately seeking hers again, grinding against their softness, until she whimpered with pain and tasted blood.

'Not like this, Kemp,' she gasped, trying to push him away, but his weight kept her where she was. She had felt him harden with that very first kiss and knew that soon it would be too late to stop anything.

Already her clothes were being removed, torn from her body. Even her stockings were expertly stripped from her legs.

'Valli . . .' He used the name to increase her humiliation as he looked down at her. 'Beautiful Valli . . . my own angel-whore.'

'You'll make me hate you,' she warned.

Still he looked down at the slim white length of her body and the growing sensual awareness in his eyes brought a shamed heat to her cheeks. He saw it and smiled derisively.

'This is the first time I've seen you blush, Valli,'

he taunted softly. 'I didn't think you could.'

His head was lowered again, his face filling her vision, and Valentine's lips parted.

It was as it had been when they had danced earlier. Kemp's caresses were deliberately insulting; he was aware only of his own driving urgency, and Valentine's anguished protests and futile struggles were overcome with offensive ease. Her jewellery grazed her smooth skin. The covering of the bed was soft beneath her naked body and above her was the hard warmth of the man who was deliberately destroying her in revenge for what had happened to his cousin. She felt as if her heart was breaking, shattering into a million bleeding fragments, never to be whole again.

Gradually, though, his lovemaking, however violent, was having its inevitable effect, and an intense burning shame added itself to her pain. How could she still want him when he was doing this to her in mockery and in scorn?

Valentine was gasping, no longer as a result of fighting him, but with the effort it cost her to conceal her mounting desire. His lips ravaged the swelling sensitivity of her breasts and she felt the blood thicken in her veins. The warmth of the summer night was turned to torrid heat and finally she could no longer resist the erotic longings he was arousing in her.

'Kemp!' It was a hoarse cry as she arched invitingly against him, flinging her arms round his neck in wild abandon, her fingers burying themselves in his hair.

'You're beautiful,' he told her carelessly. 'Beautiful and passionate, and I want you.'

His stroking, caressing hands were seeking and finding the secret untouched regions of her body, their touch maddening her, and when he paused to remove his own clothes she moaned impatiently and gasped when she saw the masculine beauty of his lean body.

'I shall go insane,' she sobbed despairingly, her hips gyrating sensuously against him.

'And why not?' he derided. 'Poetic justice, Valentine
. . . Valli! You drove Philip insane, didn't you?'

It was as if a cold wind had torn through the room,
chilling her frenzied ardour. She tried to push him away
from her now even as she felt him parting her legs, knowing that in another minute it would be too late.

'For pity's sake, Kemp, not this way,' she beseeched,
struggling to escape him once more.

'What a girl you are for changing your mind!' Kemp
said savagely.

'You can't do this!' Valentine insisted. 'You're . . .
you're too civilised, Kemp. You can't really want it to
happen this way . . . in hatred.'

'Civilised!' He laughed, but he had drawn away from
her a little.

'Please!' she went on, hating having to beg, ashamed of
being in a position of weakness. 'What would it be, like
this, save an animal coupling? I know you, I recognised
you the first time I saw you . . . You don't really want it
to happen like this! You can't!'

Abruptly Kemp rolled away from her and sat on the
edge of the bed.

'What makes you think you know me so well, my dear?'
he asked silkily.

'I just do.' She shifted her aching body and searched
his face with eyes that were still glazed from the passion
she had experienced. He looked back at her expectantly
and she saw that his eyes were hard and hot and brilliant
against the strange shadows that suddenly lay all over his
face. Beads of perspiration moistened his skin and his
mouth more than ever before gave the impression of being
twisted by some private mental pain. 'There are other
methods of revenge, Kemp,' she said quietly.

He stood up, not bothering to hide his body from her,
and found the torn black dress. 'Cover yourself,' he said
curtly, flinging it at her.

Valentine was too exhausted, both emotionally and
physically, to do more than drape it over her nakedness,

and it slipped at once, revealing the stiff rosy peak of one white breast.

'I so damned nearly took you by force,' Kemp reflected bitingly as he dressed swiftly.

'Yes.' And although he had not done so, she still felt as if her bruised body had been violated.

He sat on the edge of the bed to deal with his shoes and then turned to look at her, deliberately laying a hand flat against the inside of her knee. Valentine stirred uneasily, the desire that had so recently shaken her still too close.

'And even with the colour of humiliation in your cheeks and even though you were reduced to pleading, still you didn't weep,' he said reflectively, removing his hand.

'Nor will I ever,' she assured him tonelessly.

'What are you made of, Valentine?' he went on musingly, lips still twisting ironically. 'There's all that fatal beauty, the bewitching personality, the intense pride ... But what lies behind the great act?'

It cost her dearly to smile, but she managed it, and malice lurked in her eyes as she resumed that act.

'Someone you'll never see now, Kemp. So you'd better watch yourself, hadn't you?' She arched a delicate eyebrow. 'I might do to you what I did to Philip—only deliberately this time.'

'I thought you said you knew me,' he countered, getting up and walking round to the foot of the bed where he stood staring broodingly down at the alluring spectacle of her half-covered body. 'If you did, you'd know you can't break me. But what does it take to break you, my lovely bitch? Or do you only bend?'

'Right,' she confirmed tartly. 'And that only very occasionally.'

'Tonight being one such occasion?' he prompted cruelly.

'Ah, yes!' she flung the words at him with bright emphasis. 'Tonight you ... you diminished me, Kemp, you reduced me. But that's as much revenge as I'll ever allow you to take. Before God, I swear this is the last time you'll see me this way. From now on you can do and say what you like to me, but never again will I be . . . bent by you, Kemp Irvine.'

'I shall be interested to see how you avoid it,' he said pleasantly, and turned and left her.

Valentine got up and went to lock the door as soon as it had closed behind him. From its other side came his laughter.

'That's unnecessary, my dear,' his voice assured her. 'Next time I make love to you it will be because you want me to.'

'You'll wait a long time for that day,' she promised him.

He laughed again and she heard him depart, but he didn't go in the direction of his own bedroom, and she wondered where he was going.

A deep fatigue was dragging her down, causing her shoulders to droop, as she stood in front of the dressing-table mirror and stared at the reflected image of her pale body, youthfully slender and shockingly beautiful. Almost, she could hate Kemp for the callous treatment he had meted out to its curves and hollows. He had abused its untouched loveliness. But then a certain sense of fairness reminded her that, to an extent, his driving anger had been justified.

She should have told him about her connection with Philip long ago, she realised regretfully. It had been both stupid and selfish not to do so, and she had her punishment now in being left to wile away the long sleepless night in wondering what other methods of revenge he was contemplating.

In the morning it was an effort to drag her aching body up against the pillows and drink the coffee Maude brought her. When she got up and discovered the bruises that had developed overnight she felt mingled shock and shame: what sort of woman was she, to be able to provoke such violence in a man?

She had to select an outfit that would cover the discoloration of her shoulders, and chose a white wrap-around skirt and a short-sleeved pink cheesecloth blouse. Kemp acknowledged the departure from her usual revealing style with a lift of his eyebrows when she joined him in the breakfast room.

'Have you decided that, after all, it's dangerous to play the temptress?'

'No. I'm dressed like this out of consideration for you,' she informed him sweetly as she sat down. 'I didn't think you'd want to see the bruises and be reminded of your behaviour last night.'

He smiled twistedly. 'Then definitely it's dangerous for you to tempt me, Valentine. I don't usually mark my women.'

'I'm not your woman.' Her eyes challenged him.

'Not yet,' he conceded blandly.

'As I told you last night, you'll wait a long time,' she warned him sharply. 'Like for ever.'

'Perhaps if Philip had been prepared to wait, you'd have been his woman eventually,' Kemp suggested pointedly.

Valentine finished pouring her coffee before saying acidly, 'I suppose that from now on, Philip's name is going to be dragged into our every conversation.'

'And it hurts?' he enquired sardonically.

'I'm not a monster, Kemp,' she advised him.

'Philip's death gave you that image, though. Tell me exactly what happened, Valentine,' he invited her silkily.

'Must I?' she asked tartly. 'Are you merely curious or——'

'I want to know how it was,' he interrupted tautly. 'He was my cousin; I was out of the country at the time. I have a right to know and surely you'd rather I heard it from your lips?'

'I suppose you do have the right,' she admitted fairly, but her mouth turned down distastefully at the corners when she paused to assemble her thoughts. 'What do you want to know, though, damn you? I've told you how we

were seeing each other and that I never for one moment
guessed that he was falling in love with me. Even when
he kissed me . . . But I suppose I was controlling the situation then.'

'As I imagine you've done with most of the men in
your life,' Kemp inserted derogatively.

'Strong woman or weak men?' she retaliated swiftly.

'An element of both, I should think,' he responded
suavely.

'Thank you.' Her eyes flashed.

'Go on,' he prompted her. 'About Philip . . .?'

'Oh, hell! What more is there to explain?' Valentine
demanded resentfully. 'All right! It was a Sunday and
it was very windy, I remember, so we'd stayed in my flat
all afternoon, reading and listening to records . . . We
liked the same music. Towards evening we started talking about the change in the weather, as people do, wondering what it meant and whether it would last. I hadn't
had the flat long and I said I wondered if it wouldn't
perhaps be miserable in winter, being on the cold side
of the mountain. That was when Philip said, right out
of the blue, that actually he'd been thinking about
things and had decided we ought to look for somewhere else to live, rather than his moving in there with
me.'

'Yes?' Kemp urged expressionlessly when she was
rendered silent by the welter of pain that always accompanied the memory.

Valentine swallowed painfully and lifted her head.
'Well, I was shocked . . . I couldn't believe that he'd read
so much into our companionship and a few kisses. God,
but I was stupid!'

'Or simply young.'

'Both. I'll never underestimate what I can do to people
again,' she swore bitterly before gaining control of herself
once more. 'As I say, I was shocked, too shocked to think
before I spoke——'

'Unusual for you,' Kemp commented grimly.

'I've changed a lot since then, believe me,' she retorted with a tight little smile.

'What did you say to Philip?'

'As I remember now, I said something like, "But, Philip, I'm not in love with you," and——' Valentine came to another halt and her lips framed a silent expletive.

Kemp's eyes, never leaving her face, only added to the strain of the ordeal. He watched her impassively, but Valentine knew he was judging her—condemning her for ever as a heartless bitch, devoid of sensitivity.

'It was thoughtlessness, nothing more,' she said suddenly, desperately needing his belief. 'Thoughtlessness and the determination not to settle for less than I wanted. I didn't want Philip, I didn't love him.'

Kemp's expression didn't alter. Not even his eyes flickered at the raw urgency in her voice.

'You haven't finished yet,' he reminded her inscrutably. 'What was Philip's immediate reaction to that cruelly explicit rejection? What did he say?'

Valentine drew a resigned breath and told him sardonically, 'He said a million things, believe me. Often he said the same thing over and over again. I couldn't get him out of the flat until nearly midnight. He went on and on—I had to love him, I must love him, because he loved me. He even cried. He tried everything except your tactics of last night. I know it sounds a terrible thing to say, but he nagged me. I was exhausted. He was like a child who becomes hysterical when he can't get his own way . . . I'll hold my breath until you give it to me. I couldn't believe it was Philip behaving that way. I'd never seen that side of him before.'

Kemp nodded and now there was a certain grimness about his expression. 'And when did you find out about Rose's existence?'

'Some time during that evening,' she confessed flatly. 'Suddenly, in the midst of all his other arguments, he said how could I do this to him when he'd already told his wife there was someone else and moved out of the house they had in Gardens? I was appalled ... Perhaps I was also hysterical by that stage, because I remember thinking it was terribly, ironically, funny that her name should be Rose because that's also my second name. She must have had a romantic mother too.'

'I think you're slightly hysterical now as well,' Kemp said sharply. 'Go on, Valentine, you haven't told me the end yet.'

'Shylock!' she accused. Her eyes darkened and the knuckles of the hand holding her coffee cup were white as she took a sip. 'For a week Philip didn't leave me alone. He'd be waiting for me after work and for the rest of the evening he'd argue, attempting to persuade me ... I didn't know what to do and probably a lot of the things I said only aggravated the state he was in. I tried anger and sympathy, I tried reasoning, I tried to persuade him to go back to his wife ... By the end of the week his mood had become one of juvenile spitefulness: the I'll-make-you-sorry syndrome. On the Sunday I drove down to Gordon's Bay just to get a few hours of peace. My brother was at home and he said clearly Philip needed professional help, and I went back determined to persuade him to see someone. He was waiting outside the flat. At first I thought he was only drunk because I could smell alcohol, and I was afraid that at last he was going to resort to violence ... He didn't make a lot of sense and it was some time before I understood that he'd taken something else as well. He threatened me then. He said since I wouldn't love him, he'd make my name dirt in Cape Town. He'd written explanations to Rose and to his parents, telling them just why he was doing what he did ... Those letters were used at the inquest. I telephoned for help, but of course it was too late. The combination of alcohol and drugs ... I don't know! Perhaps he didn't really want to die and was trying to blackmail me, but then I don't think he'd have written those letters. I just don't know.'

'Neither do I, Valentine,' Kemp said shortly. 'I wish I

did. Philip was ... Philip! And you were left to face an inquest?'

She cast him a smoulderingly resentful look. 'Yes! So there's no need for you to be planning revenge, you see, because I suffered enough then ... suffered humiliation and guilt and the naked feeling that comes with notoriety. Fortunately the various official people conducting the investigation had seen enough of life's sordidness to treat me sympathetically and without blame, but how could Philip's parents be expected to understand my side of the matter? Or Rose? She didn't attend the inquest, but I imagine she hates me as much as Philip's parents did. And then there was the press—not the responsible press for which I have the greatest admiration, but the sensational press, hacks who can write the truth and still give a more scandalous impression. With the help of my so-called friends, they turned me into a Jezebel ... or do I mean a Delilah? It made their day when Philip's mother attacked me after the inquest, screaming that I'd killed him. She made me feel guilty ... I could have understood him better, I could have done more sooner instead of waiting until my brother told me what to do. But I didn't understand, you see.'

'Bitterness is pointless, Valentine,' Kemp advised her abruptly. 'Edward wrote to me a couple of times telling me how it was all but destroying Reinette. Perhaps it was merciful that she didn't have to go on living too long, haunted by the knowledge of what had become of her only son.'

'I don't require underlinings, Kemp,' Valentine flared sharply. 'God! Imagine if she knew I was at Fleurmont.'

'I said bitterness achieves nothing,' Kemp repeated furiously.

But he had wanted to hurt her, she knew. That was why he had so relentlessly extracted the whole sordid story from her. She was afraid that she had revealed too much while telling it, thereby giving him another weapon to use against her in his quest for revenge. He would know now that whenever he wanted to cause her pain, he had only to mention his cousin.

Whatever thoughts her story had given rise to, they seemed to be occupying Kemp fully, and they finished breakfast in silence.

When they stood up to go outside, Valentine asked, 'May I telephone Adam Ducaine and ask him to join us at dinner tonight?'

He smiled, eyeing her contemplatively. 'You're a strange, resilient creature, Valentine.'

'I've had to be.'

'You weren't always this way?' he probed.

'Before Philip, do you mean?' she lashed out. 'No, until that happened I was a normal, ordinary person.'

'Normal, possibly, but never, ever ordinary,' he contradicted her. 'You never wept for Philip, did you?'

'I told you yesterday: I hate him for what he did to me,' she said levelly. 'It was immature and quite deliberate . . . His coming to my flat, the letters mentioning my name . . . They all prove it, don't they? It was his revenge because I couldn't love him.'

'Where is pity, Valentine?' he asked softly.

'I have none.'

'Then you're less than a whole woman,' he told her contemptuously.

But she did pity Philip; only to admit it would make Kemp see just how truly vulnerable she was.

'You haven't answered my question,' she reminded him as they stepped outside and the morning sunlight struck them. 'May I invite Adam?'

'Why do you want him?' he enquired with deceptive mildness. 'Can it be that you're afraid of being alone with me in the evenings?'

Her exquisite chin lifted. 'You're the one who should be afraid, Kemp—of me, and the curse I hold for men!'

'You fool!'

'I like Adam's company, that's all. And don't worry:

he's too fond of himself ever to suffer over me the way Philip did.'

'Tell him Emma is included in the invitation,' Kemp adjured lightly, his eyes glinting.

'She'll be delighted,' Valentine said brightly.

He laughed. 'You don't sound the same way, sweetheart. I know you dislike her, but I have strong objections to being a solitary third while you ... entertain her brother.'

'A desire to entertain is one of the lesser reasons for my wanting him to come to dinner,' she told him in a honeyed voice.

'Then I hate to think what the major reasons are.' He paused and looked about him, his restless gaze encompassing everything: the shining blue sky above the serene mountains, the flower-smothered foothills, the vineyards and the historic buildings about them. 'Time to harvest the grapes. All this is something for which I suppose I have you to thank. God! I'd give a lot to be a thousand miles away from both you and Fleurmont, Valentine.'

She spread her hands, looking at him curiously. 'I'm sorry. I know how tied you feel.' She hesitated. 'If it's not the right life for you, you could sell or become an absentee owner. You don't have to be here.'

But Kemp was shaking his head, his eyes going now to the old slave bell. 'Slavery still exists today in various forms. Most of us become slaves to responsibility.'

He walked away from her then and Valentine looked after him, recognising the frustration he felt. It was wrong, all wrong, she thought, but she was helpless to remedy the situation. She didn't even have the right to advise him, and if she attempted to do so, he would treat her suggestions with contempt. But a man like Kemp shouldn't be tied in this way.

During the course of the day she telephoned the Ducaine estate. Adam accepted her invitation with delighted alacrity and thought Emma would do so too.

'She has a mad crush on Kemp,' he laughed.

'I had noticed,' Valentine said drily.

Emma occupied her mind at odd moments of the day. Was it mere adoration that she felt for Kemp, or was she a woman intent on winning what she had set her heart on, by any means? To what lengths would she go? Valentine kept hearing Adam's voice as it had sounded last Saturday——' . . . she suddenly took it into her head to go down to Cape Town this morning . . .'

Valentine knew Emma regarded her as a rival. That envelope containing the newspaper cuttings had been posted in Cape Town, but would it have taken so long to get here if the obscured date was Saturday's? But she could have asked someone else to post it for her later—

Valentine just couldn't be sure. And from whose sordid scrapbook had those cuttings come? How had Emma, if she was responsible, got hold of them? Somehow she couldn't imagine the squeaky clean girl as the owner of such a collection. Only the sad and the lonely, those whose excitement in life must be vicarious, found entertainment in such stories.

Later she spoke to Salome Jansen. 'Adam and Emma Ducaine are coming to dinner, Salome. I hope you don't mind?'

'Of course not. But I thought you'd have given that Adam up by now?' Salome's shiny brown eyes regarded her speculatively. 'He's no good to a girl like you. But you and Mr Irvine have quarrelled, haven't you?'

'Not exactly quarrelled,' Valentine said carefully. She thought for a moment, then straightened her shoulders. 'But he's found out the truth about me, you see. I suppose the rest of you have the right to know: I'm the girl who was involved with Philip de Villiers at the time of his death.'

She waited for the revulsion to chase the smile from Salome's face, but the woman merely shrugged. 'So? I knew that, *skatjie*, but since you didn't mention it, neither did I.'

'You knew?' Valentine felt laughter bubbling up inside her.

'Sure. My memory isn't that short.' Salome shrugged again. 'Anyway, that Philip ... I'll tell you a secret. I didn't like him. He treated us employees as if his family was doing us a favour, but how would Fleurmont continue to function without people like Freddie and Maude and me, I'd like to know? It was a tragedy for everyone, of course, but you were right not to yield to the pressure he was obviously applying. He was a weak one. A strong, spirited girl like you needs a real man ... someone like Mr Irvine!'

And I know it, Valentine thought sadly.

CHAPTER SIX

THE last visitors that day were a party of Australians and their South African hosts, and since they were from Australia's own wine-producing region, they answered as well as asked questions, appreciating Valentine's reciprocal interest. Finally, she laughingly refused their various invitations to dinner, waved to them as they departed and made sure that Maude had removed the glasses before going across to the house.

Kemp was headed the same way, coming from the office, at the same time as Emma drove up in her little red car.

'She's very early if she's come to dinner,' Valentine commented amusedly, having crossed swiftly to Kemp's side. 'I suppose she just couldn't wait to see you.'

He smiled at her mimicry of Emma's voice. 'Sometimes I wonder why we apply the word bitch to women like you, sweetheart. You're much more like a cat, all claws and malice and sensuality.'

'That's probably why I adore cats, darling,' she said lightly.

'Do you? There's something I want to tell you about a cat some day, but it will keep.'

'Yes, we must go and welcome our guest,' she agreed facetiously. 'Do you mind if I hold your arm?'

'I don't mind,' he replied meaningly. 'But I do wonder why you should want to.'

Valentine clapped one dramatic hand to her brow, curved the other round Kemp's arm at the level of his elbow and swayed like a graceful willow on her high heels. 'Suddenly, quite suddenly, you understand, I feel faint.'

He laughed, his eyes gleaming. 'What an act, ranging from high tragedy to pure farce! What are you like when you're not giving a performance?'

She met his eyes with a wickedly mysterious look in her own. 'This one isn't for your benefit, Kemp.'

'Emma's, of course?' he guessed smoothly.

Valentine gave the other girl an assessing look as she got out of her car.

'Now there's one bitch who's all bitch,' she murmured suddenly, her fingers tightening against the warm inside hollow of his elbow.

'Emma?'

'No, silly!' She laughed delicately. 'Emma is a very nice girl who'd make a good wife for a wine farmer. I meant that dog of hers.'

'Queenie?' He glanced at the fat golden spaniel who accompanied Emma. 'She's a harmless old lump.'

'She loathes me.' Valentine smiled up at him quite brilliantly. 'She probably senses Emma's dislike of me and reacts accordingly. Dogs can be quite stupidly loyal, can't they? Incidentally, I found out today that Salome has known who I was all along.'

'She's a shrewd woman. I take it you don't suspect her of having sent those newspaper cuttings?'

'Oh, no, of course not.' Valentine widened her eyes and turned them on the approaching Emma, and she heard Kemp draw a sharp breath.

'Behave yourself,' he muttered warningly.

She gave him another meltingly innocent smile which Emma noted with a pout. Her wide grey eyes looked hurt as she reached them, but she spoke cheerfully enough: 'Hullo, Kemp. I thought I'd come over early and get a ride on Undine.' She indicated the vanity case she was carrying and the riding clothes in which she was clad. 'And you'll ride Oriel, won't you? Adam will be over later, Valentine.'

'Adam?' Valentine looked vague as she slowly moved her slender fingers caressingly up and down Kemp's inside elbow, making sure Emma had noticed before desisting. If the girl was in fact responsible for those newspaper cuttings, she was not going to have the satisfaction of knowing the harm they had caused. 'Oh, Adam! Of course. My mind was on other things. Kemp and I have just stopped work for the day. Why is that animal growling at me?'

'She won't hurt you,' Emma said scornfully. 'Not if you don't show your fear.'

'She certainly does seem to dislike you,' Kemp commented amusedly.

'I can't understand it,' Emma said guilelessly. 'She likes absolutely everyone else. They're odd, intelligent creatures, dogs ... They have an uncanny instinct for the truth about people.'

Valentine looked at her speculatively from beneath her long eyelashes. To what truth was Emma referring?

'Can't you control her, Emma?' Kemp asked. 'I don't think you've ever given her much training, have you?'

'Oh, I know!' Emma smiled deprecatingly as the dog's growls subsided. 'I suppose I'm just too soft.'

'Like a marshmallow?' Valentine asked interestedly, and Emma looked hurt, her bottom lip quivering as she looked appealingly at Kemp.

'She's just trying to get you to join the club, Emma,' he said dismissively. 'I once called her a meringue.'

Emma giggled. 'But why, Kemp?'

'Oh!'

It was from Valentine that the exclamation came. Unnoticed by any of them, Queenie had silently circled them until she was behind Valentine, when she proceeded to gently fasten her teeth round the smooth curve of her leg just above the ankle.

'Queenie!' At the sound of Kemp's voice, Queenie bolted in the direction of Rufus and Chet who had just appeared. 'Are you all right, Valli?'

'Yes. I got a fright, that's all,' she said a little shakily, standing precariously on one leg and looking over her shoulder at the other for signs of injury. Kemp crouched beside her to examine it, running his fingers lightly over the faintly throbbing area, and Valentine steadied herself by placing a hand on his shoulder.

She glanced sharply at Emma, noted the perplexed dissatisfaction marring her face, and knew that Kemp's use of the old name was responsible. Valentine bit down hard on an irresistible smile. Poor Emma! She could pity her even in the midst of her growing conviction that the girl had been responsible for sending those press cuttings.

'The skin isn't broken.' Kemp released her leg, straightening up, and Valentine clutched his arm again, smiling demurely at him and registering the sharp amusement glinting in his eyes. 'You really should do something about that dog, Emma.'

Emma looked sulky. 'I don't know what Valentine is making such a fuss about,' she said loftily. 'As you said, the skin isn't even broken.'

Valentine's eyes flew open. 'But I'm not making a fuss, Emma,' she denied gently and truthfully. 'But it was very . . . sly of your dog, wasn't it? Underhand, in a sense, to sneak round behind me instead of attacking openly. Our dogs wouldn't do it that way, would they, Kemp? But then they've nicer natures than Queenie.'

'Possibly because they're males,' Kemp suggested drily, and his quick glance warned her that he thought she was going too far.

Valentine leaned against him deliberately, watching the spectacle of Emma's chagrin. The girl's acutely uncomfortable reaction to her use of certain words had confirmed her suspicions.

'Why don't you two go and have your ride now, darling?' she suggested smoothly. 'I'll take your little case inside, Emma.'

'You won't join us?' Kemp invited as she released his arm. 'You ride Idun, don't you?'

'As Emma will certainly tell you, if I don't, I couldn't keep up with you, Kemp,' she explained easily, taking the vanity case from the girl's nerveless fingers. 'I'll have drinks waiting for you when you return.'

'Your riding has made so little progress in six months, Valentine,' Emma said spitefully. 'You're really a city girl, aren't you? Country life doesn't seem to suit you.'

'Goodness, Emma, you always talk as if we were living in the real bundu,' Valentine said, feigning amused surprise. 'As a matter of fact, life here in the wine region is more civilised and sophisticated than anything I've been accustomed to.'

Emma scowled. 'Come on, Kemp, let's go,' she said impatiently.

She was stalking away and Valentine looked at Kemp with sparkling eyes, her mouth shaping the words, 'Thank you.'

He shook his head slightly, his lips twisting. 'I'll accept your thanks some other time, Valli. Remember that.'

Then he was following Emma, and Valentine went slowly towards the house, making a wide circle round Queenie who, with the other dogs, had reappeared, and wondering if Rufus and Chet would leap to her defence if the bitch attacked her again.

Once inside, she forgot the dogs. Just why had Kemp chosen to support the act she had put on for Emma's benefit? Valentine felt a little uneasy. It must have been in line with some purpose of his own to do it, otherwise he would have refused to play—but what?

Emma's presence had implanted in her a mischievous desire to appear at her most exotic that evening, but when she stripped and stepped into the shower she realised that the bruises on her shoulders had not yet faded, so shoe-string straps were out of the question. In the end, after much deliberation, she donned a dress of oyster georgette, her favourite fabric, carefully twisting and turning in front of the mirror to make sure that the cleavage revealing vee-neck didn't disclose any bruises. Her shoulders, though, were covered, since the dress had loose sleeves ending just above the elbow; about her slender waist she clasped a wide gold belt to match her high sandals; and the skirt was a graceful thing of soft folds ending at her knees. It had been designed to be worn with a petticoat of some sort, but Valentine disliked the effect of rigging showing through its semi-transparency, and went bra-less as well so that the dark tips of her breasts were occasionally visible and when she stood in the light the entire outline of her figure was revealed.

Adam Ducaine had arrived by the time she drifted along the passage to the hall, taking her time and breathing appreciatively the fragrance of Yves St Laurent's Opium which she often wore, deriving a purely sensuous pleasure from both it and the smooth soft touch of her dress against her skin. It was so light, and so were her sandals, and she played with the fancy that she was weightless, floating along—

Kemp met her in the hall. 'I was coming to look for you,' he said, and then—'Lead me away and lay me down! We're going to have fun tonight. Is that for Adam's benefit?'

Valentine tilted her head, saying facetiously, 'Am I to gather that you appreciate my subtle allure?'

'Subtle!' he laughed. 'It's a good thing some of my television colleagues aren't around to see you. Subtle isn't the word they'd use ... But all right, subtle in one sense, sweetheart, but in another sense, definitely not.'

She was pleased with the impact she had made. It added to her confidence and truly, the soft shade was subtle, and the only truly flamboyant colour about her was the red of her lips and nails.

'In fact, I thought the whole effect rather bridal,' she murmured, touching the tiny artificial flowers of stiff oyster-coloured silk which nestled against the dark curls at the back of her head. A few extra tendrils were allowed to frame her face and tiny gold studs adorned her earlobes.

'Bridal? In my experience, that of an observer only, I hasten to add, brides are generally concealed from head to toe, whereas you're not hiding a thing.' His amused blue eyes travelled over her from head down to scarlet toenails, lingering longest over those areas which the dress covered but didn't conceal. 'But what subconscious yearnings can have brought such an image to your mind? Do you believe in marriage, Valentine?'

'Definitely!' She gave him a dazzling smile. 'As I told you last night, I'm the last of the great idealists.'

'Happily-ever-after and all that?' he derided.

'Not quite, but a travelling on together, two people growing and learning from each other, perhaps having a child or two, but remaining primarily husband and wife even when they become parents . . .' Her voice died away and she wondered if she had said too much. To admit to a belief in marriage was perhaps to give him yet one more weapon to use against her in his self-confessed quest for revenge.

'Who would have believed it?' Kemp drawled.

Valentine forced the sparkle back into her eyes and fluttered her eyelashes. 'Adam and Emma will be wondering what's keeping us . . . Emma especially. Shall we join them?'

'I can't wait to see Adam's face.'

Adam's reaction would have proved gratifying had Valentine noticed it, but it was Emma who interested her, and she saw the girl's shock, followed by a look incorporating both jealousy and hatred, and felt a mixture of amusement and regret. It was something she was accustomed to, the dislike of other women, and while she occasionally wished it could be otherwise, she knew that female nature would never change. Besides, Emma looked very pretty in her lemon yellow chiffon—and anyway, Valentine reminded herself, she deserved to suffer a little if she was the person who had posted those newspaper cuttings to Kemp. Why couldn't she have told him to his face?

While her own suffering as a result of the situation that had arisen out of her own cowardice was never far from the surface, Valentine possessed a natural resilience, plus a conviction that all things had to be endured, however

painful, and she enjoyed the evening. Just the sound of
Kemp's beautiful voice could give her pleasure, but he
was also an intelligent, sophisticated and interesting host
once again, and Adam too, with his polished suavity, fitted
into the milieu with the utmost ease.

When she had invited Adam to dinner, Valentine had
intended questioning him in an attempt to find out if
Emma could possibly be the person responsible for sending those cuttings. Now she no longer felt the need to do
so, since she was virtually sure of it. Nevertheless, when
Adam, with his sister's rather obvious approval, suggested that he and Valentine go outside 'for a stroll' as
he platitudinously put it, she accepted with an enquiring
lift of one eyebrow when she saw Kemp's sardonic
smile.

She let Adam hold her hand and they walked in the
garden for a while until she made an excuse about her
dress being too thin to make the night air pleasant. He
wanted to put his arms round her and warm her then,
and a wish to kiss her naturally followed, but she turned
her head so that his lips only met the smoothness of her
cheek.

'You'll smudge my lipstick,' she said lightly, pouting a
little, and he sighed resignedly. 'Let's go in. I'm sure that
hound of your sister's is lurking about somewhere, waiting
to attack me!'

Emma was sitting beside Kemp on the sofa—it had
been Valentine's place—looking soft-eyed and very
pleased with herself when they went in, and Valentine's
red lips puckered in amusement. Kemp dealt very gently
with the girl, but she was almost sure his interest in Emma
was minimal. When he loved it would be someone as
strong as he was, and worthy of him, and he was not the
man to contemplate a match simply because it was suit-
able.

Her own exchanges with Kemp won a hawklike observ-
ance from Emma, Valentine noticed, and not without
cause: she was in one of her best social moods tonight and

he was not averse to letting her have her head, although she suspected there was a reckoning to come. It was strange, but now that Kemp knew the appalling truth about her, she felt more confident in his company. She had nothing left to hide from him—except her pain.

Later, long after Salome and Maude had retired to their quarters for the night, Valentine stood up gracefully.

'Shall I make some more coffee?' Sympathetically, she noticed Emma's resentment of her adoption of the hostess's rôle. 'Come and help me, Emma.'

A warning glance came from Kemp as she passed him, but Valentine merely shook her head slightly, smiling faintly.

In the kitchen Emma silently gave her a little half-hearted assistance, then stood and watched her unhappily.

'You can stop wondering, Emma,' Valentine said eventually, giving her a direct look. 'Yes, Kemp did receive your sordid little contribution to the truth.'

'I . . . I don't know what you're talking about,' Emma muttered, flushing deeply.

'It's been exercising your mind all evening, hasn't it?' Valentine went on coldly. 'You couldn't understand why, if he knew the truth, I should still be here . . . Well, thanks to you, he does now know the truth, but as you've observed for yourself, it hasn't changed a thing.'

'I don't believe you. If he knew, he'd hate you . . .' Emma's voice died.

'One thing worries me,' Valentine continued, uninterested in the girl's reaction. 'From whose scrapbook did those cuttings come? Not yours, surely?'

'All right, I'll tell you,' Emma granted with sudden viciousness. 'I've an old great-aunt in Cape Town who takes an interest in such things, scandals . . . I had a look through her collection once. That's why, after a while, I realised who you were. I put them in an envelope when I visited her last Saturday and she was to post them for me. I suppose you even stoop to intercepting mail——'

'Kemp has seen them,' Valentine interrupted quietly. 'Why, Emma?'

'Why?' Emma flung out a hand. 'Look at you, dressed like a tart, flaunting yourself ... You're no good for Kemp. You'll take him away from Fleurmont . . . I'll do anything to free him from you. You'd destroy him as you did Philip de Villiers.'

'The woman isn't breathing who can destroy Kemp Irvine,' Valentine stated with proud conviction.

'I don't understand what men see in you,' Emma rushed on tearfully. 'You're . . . you look cheap!'

'Perhaps you simply don't understand men,' Valentine suggested. 'Listen to me, Emma. I am ... me. I display the assets I was granted by nature to their best advantage or I become a hypocrite. But it's not always easy or pleasant. Women often share your opinion regarding the way I look; men don't.'

'I bet they all think you're easy, though,' Emma said spitefully. 'And you probably are.'

'Strangely enough, most men accord me a certain degree of respect,' Valentine said with a shrug. 'People value you by the value you place on yourself, you know. Come, the coffee is ready and since you're not prepared to listen to me, we may as well end this discussion.'

'I'll tell Kemp how ... how horrible you've been to me,' Emma threatened.

'Do,' Valentine advised contemptuously, and led the way back to the sitting-room.

But Emma didn't tell him. Instead, by means of look and manner she made it clear that she had had her feelings hurt, and Kemp was very kind to her.

Later, having seen the brother and sister off in their separate cars, Queenie accompanying Emma, Valentine said to Kemp as he locked the front door: 'I enjoyed this evening. I'm afraid Emma didn't, though, poor sweet.'

He turned to look at her. 'Thanks to you.'

She shook her head. 'You're going to hurt that girl, Kemp.'

'As you hurt Philip?' he taunted. 'No, Valli, Emma is like her brother. She has a natural regard for herself.'

'Oh, she won't be destroyed, I'll grant you.' Valentine's mouth was pulled into a tragic line as his mention of Philip brought pain close to the surface. 'But she'll still suffer.'

'It's one of life's nastier little surprises, isn't it?' he drawled. 'Finding oneself responsible for someone else's happiness and unable to become what they want you to be.'

'Isn't it just?' she agreed bitterly.

'There speaks the voice of terrible experience,' he mocked lightly.

'Don't you want to know what passed between Emma and me in the kitchen?' she changed the subject pointedly.

'I can guess,' he retorted impatiently. 'You gained confirmation of certain suspicions you'd been harbouring . . . So what the hell, Valentine? I had to learn the truth somehow or other, since you weren't prepared to divulge it and that way was probably as good as any.'

'I beg to differ,' she said icily. 'I found it a particularly unpleasant manner of bringing the truth to light.'

'Then you should have told me yourself, right at the beginning, right?' Kemp ground out harshly. 'Why the hell didn't you?'

Valentine squared her shoulders and produced a bright artifical smile. 'Because I was frightened, you see,' she stated in her clear beautiful voice. 'Yes, even I . . . Or perhaps I wanted to make you like me first, I wanted to win something from you. Giving you the Valentine card was enough. I was going to tell you at lunchtime. It's all right, Kemp, I don't expect you to believe that, but I swear it's true.'

'I'm relieved by the return of your unique directness,' he mocked, his lips twisting. 'But such candour could turn back on you, sweetheart. You're really setting yourself up, aren't you?'

'To be shot down? What does it matter?' Bitterness was

a corrosive thing, causing her to lash out, but it was herself she was whipping. 'You already have plenty of weapons to use against me. One more can't make any difference.'

'Can't it?'

'Oh, I've no doubt you'll endeavour to make sure it does make a difference. I could hate you, Kemp,' she went on with hopelessness deadening her beautiful eyes. 'I'll never believe I was more than just a little to blame for a young man's emotional imbalance, but don't you think I've suffered enough, without your contribution towards punishing me?'

'You're the one who's doing the punishing, Valentine,' he told her tautly. 'I wonder when you'll realise it? Go to bed now. It's late and I don't feel like arguing with you. You needn't lock your door.'

'I know that. You wouldn't let yourself be provoked the same way twice, would you, Kemp?' she taunted, resenting the steely strength of will which gave him such power.

'Well, not in precisely the same way,' he agreed, and a certain grimly humorous inflection had entered his voice. 'Nevertheless, you are a provocative woman ... Valli! Quite extravagantly so.'

He was looking at her in such a way that her red lips parted involuntarily and a still, expectant tension held her body immobile. She stood with the light behind her, slim and fragile, with her dark head thrown back, and Kemp's eyes moved over the smooth outlines of her figure, travelling upward from her slender thighs to where the rosy peaks of her breasts were just visible, jutting against the soft material of her dress.

'Kemp ...' It was a whisper, born of both fear and yearning.

'Relax!' His voice had all the sharp suddenness of a pistol shot. 'I'm not interested when you've already had Adam Ducaine's hands all over you tonight.'

Recovering her composure, she said, 'That's a trifle exaggerated, darling.'

'Do you really enjoy being mauled about by young men who mean nothing to you and who can do nothing for you?' he went on distastefully.

'I never permit . . . mauling, as you so crudely put it,' she assured him haughtily. A malicious little smile touched her lips. 'You told me this morning that you don't usually mark your women, Kemp. Well, you're the only man who's ever left bruises on me.'

He seemed to sigh. 'However civilised we like to think ourselves, there remains a basic primitive core in all of us, and who can predict what's going to draw it out? You succeeded where no one else has, Valentine, and you suffered for it. I was brutal, I know, and however much you deserve to suffer, you didn't merit physical violence. It won't happen again.'

'Thank you. Goodnight, Kemp.'

For a timeless moment she filled her vision with the sight of him. Her heart felt wrung, her mind almost at breaking point. He was such a beautiful man, damn him, with his height and leanness, that tanned skin and the intensely blue eyes, his almost fair hair and those hands, civilised hands which had thus shocked her with the cruelty of their caresses last night . . . Ah, God, and that ironical mouth and the network of fine lines about his eyes that she would like to touch with her lips and fingers . . .

But what enslaved her was the wholeness of him, not just his beautiful strong body and the face that looked as if it had seen all of life, but the total personality, the intelligence and humour of him. So often he unknowingly confirmed for her that initial feeling of recognition she had experienced.

'Goodnight, Valentine.'

A brief acknowledging inclination of her head, and she turned from him, departing with matchless grace, and Kemp watched her go.

Harvesting got under way and the tempo of life on the

estate quickened. The good weather held as if to deliberately thwart Freddie Jansen's pessimistic predictions that
they wouldn't finish in time.

Valentine saw less of Kemp now, for despite his lack of
inclination to be the owner of a wine estate, he made
himself as active as the other men and she realised, from
things she heard, that the Fleurmont employees all respected him.

Nevertheless, the social life of the district didn't come
to an end just because the gathering of the grapes had
begun. Singly or together, Valentine and Kemp were
often invited out to dinner or to parties.

At one such dinner party on the Ducaine estate, it
became clear to Valentine that Mrs Ducaine shared her
daughter's fears as the older woman stiffly advised her of
what she considered to be the impropriety of the situation
at Fleurmont.

'You and Kemp are alone together in that house, with
the servants' quarters apart from the main living area,'
she pointed out to a politely attentive Valentine. 'People
will talk and make suggestions, probably only in jest to
begin with, but then the rumours will start and finally
you'll find that a firm conviction has grown up regarding
what's going on.'

'And what is going on?' Valentine enquired mischievously, her eyes straying to the opposite end of the room
where a gratified Emma had all Kemp's attention.

'Oh, nothing, I'm sure, my dear,' Mrs Ducaine said
hastily, but she didn't sound very convinced. 'But you
know how it is ... The situation isn't a conventional
one.'

'I hadn't thought of it like that,' Valentine admitted.

'I suppose not. You're a rather unconventional person,
aren't you?' Mrs Ducaine definitely did not mean it as a
compliment.

'I would have thought I was par for the course ... in
this day and age,' Valentine brought out the much-used
phrase with a certain hauteur, resenting being given

advice by someone who so clearly disliked her.

'Couldn't you have a room in the Hattinghs' house?' Mrs Ducaine pressed on.

'I wouldn't wish to intrude on their family life—and Sylvie might be afraid I'd seduce James,' Valentine added wickedly, and saw the older woman's mouth purse. 'I'll have to ask Kemp what he thinks, Mrs Ducaine. You see, I think he has other plans for me.'

And with a melting smile, she rose swiftly and drifted away to talk to someone else. A sliver of ice worked its way further into her heart. She had spoken so truly: Kemp undeniably had plans for her. He intended that she should suffer, not just a single revenge, but several forms of it, and he had a plentiful supply of weapons to use against her. Just now, when he was so busy, he confined himself to barbed comments and the occasional references to Philip, so that she was never in any doubt of his contempt, but Valentine knew that later on he intended that she should truly pay, in several ways, for the tragedy that had befallen his cousin. All she could do in the meantime was gather her strength and pray that it would be sufficient to disguise from him the damage he would do. She would never let him see if he was successful, she vowed intensely.

'Do you think our situation is unconventional?' she asked him curiously on the way home. 'Mrs Ducaine thinks I should move in with the Hattinghs before people start thinking you and I are having an affair.'

'Good God!' He sounded amused. 'I hadn't thought of it in that light. How do you feel about it, Valentine? Do you mind what people say about you?'

'I've been talked about before and in a worse way,' she reminded him bitterly. 'I survived that.'

'The great survivor,' he mocked silkily. 'You are, aren't you? But you'll crack one day, my lovely.'

'If you have anything to do with it, right?' she challenged.

'I've warned you about the dangers of bitterness before,' he reminded her impatiently. After a short silence he added thoughtfully, 'All the same, this unconventional situation could give rise to many things in time.'

'A very clear threat, Kemp,' she retorted acidly.

'No. Merely a warning . . . Valli!' He brought the terrible name out harshly.

'I'm not afraid of you,' she assured him, her voice a silvery sound, full of mystery, because she wasn't emphatic at all.

'Ah, yes. What was it you swore?' he derided. 'That I'd never bend you, or make you weep? But I'll do both. I wish you'd resign yourself to that fact and stop fighting me.'

'I'll die first!'

'And you'll never die, will you? It's going to be a long campaign,' he reflected, and Valentine felt herself grow cold.

It was also during this time that two of his former colleagues from his production crew came to stay at Fleurmont for a couple of days. Valentine liked them. They were nice men, in their thirties, with a slightly ribald sense of humour, and she never minded the goodnatured passes they made at her because they accepted their rejection so cheerfully, and she came to the conclusion that they were really more interested in their work and drinking than in women. One was an inveterate chain-smoker, while the other rejected their wine disdainfully and drank only beer, lots of it.

Valentine noticed how fully Kemp entered into their conversations about work, and she realised anew that he had given himself more completely to that old life than he ever would to this business of wine-production.

Their visitors departed and the busy sunny days continued. The grapes continued to be brought in. The total crop would have to go through the de-stalking crusher before undergoing, ultimately, the entire ritual of de-juicers and pre-press; then the final press; the distilling tanks for the whites and open fermentation tanks for the reds; the vital centrifuges where the white wines were cleared and the dead yeast cells removed; the white wine fermentation tanks and the vats for the reds, the casks made of European oak, where a wine like the Cabernet would have to mature for up to nine months before being bottled.

Valentine knew the procedure off by heart because it was something she explained daily to their visitors. She was the guide on their tours right through the production cellar. Then there were the stabilising and storage tanks, the filling room with its expensive and modern equipment of rinsers, steriliser, bottler and corker, storage space where whites rested for a few months, reds for much longer, and the labelling area . . . Only the all-important tasting-room was private, hidden away from any disturbance. There the cellarmaster and vintner's palates would determine the quality of their produce.

Even Sundays were busy now. Only Valentine was off duty, and late on a Sunday morning in March she dressed herself in soft blue-grey shorts that hugged her slender waist, and a fine white shirt, and went towards the foothills, preferring to walk since taking Idun would hinder the fulfilment of her intention which was simply to relax.

The dogs accompanied her for part of the way before racing off on a pursuit of their own, and Valentine went on alone until she came to the flower-starred sweeps of grass, one of her favourite parts of Fleurmont. It was a bright, still day. The world of mountain and sky had a sunlit serenity and not a sound came to her ears as she lay down in the soft warm grass. Everyone was far, far away. She was alone and she unfastened another button of her shirt, taking sensuous pleasure in the heat of the sun. She lay motionless, staring up at the sky, while a pale yellow flower tickled the side of her neck.

So it was that Kemp found her.

CHAPTER SEVEN

'I'VE escaped for a while,' Kemp told her with a crooked smile.

Valentine raised herself on her elbows, drawing up one long smooth leg, and looked at him concernedly. 'Why don't you escape permanently?' she asked, for his frustration at being here was often on her mind.

'How can I?' He had sat down beside her and now he glanced back in the direction of the vineyards.

'You must do what's best for you personally,' she ventured carefully. 'Or rather, what you feel you must do. Once when we were talking about this, you said something about responsibility, but isn't there another, greater responsibility? That of being . . . being true to yourself? Your documentaries showed you had the ability to make people become aware, without manipulating them emotionally, and surely that's more important than the production of wine? I think it's what you believe.'

'You can see so much of me, can't you?' he queried idly. 'But Fleurmont meant so much to Edward and Reinette . . . And it would be a good place for a child to grow up.'

That last was disturbing, but she smiled calmly. 'Are you thinking of getting married?'

An ironic glint appeared in his eyes. 'Not in the immediate future, anyway.'

Relieved, she reverted to the main topic. 'You could continue to own Fleurmont and go on with your job, you know. You could come back between assignments, when you wanted a rest.'

'And you'd be here to entertain me, I suppose?' he laughed.

'Who knows where I'll be?' she countered lightly.

'I never did receive formal notice from you,' he remembered.

'No.' For a moment she was thoughtful, wondering what instinct towards self-destruction had prevented her leaving. But it would have been running away, and she prided herself on having a certain amount of courage. She gave Kemp a brilliant mocking smile. 'You haven't pushed me far enough yet.'

He smiled too. 'I'll begin to think you're a masochist.'

'No. I'm just a fool,' she sighed.

There was silence for a while, then Kemp said, 'There's something I've been meaning to tell you about Philip.'

Valentine sat up straight, the bitter light of resentment back in her eyes. 'I might have known. Now you really are pushing me too far, Kemp. You're only my employer, after all, and I'm off duty. I came here to relax in peace and look at the mountains. I didn't resent it when you arrived, but if you're going to start taunting me with Philip again——'

'Shut up and listen to me, Valli,' Kemp interrupted impatiently.

'Don't call me Valli!' she snapped, trying to stand up, but a steely grip on her arm prevented her.

'Why not? It's your name,' he taunted cruelly. 'You may be off duty, but you're on my property, so you can damn well stay and listen!'

'I suppose I've no choice,' she said resignedly.

'None at all.' Kemp released her arm and looked at her assessingly for a few seconds. Then he sighed exasperatedly. 'Although why I should bother with someone so self-absorbed and defensive, I do not know ... But for what it's worth, Philip was a difficult personality throughout his childhood. He led Edward and Reinette a hell of a life. God knows what made him the way he was. He had security, a happy family life ... Edward and Reinette were the normal sort of parents, but for some reason he was always convinced they didn't love him

enough, a belief which resulted in his applying a form of
emotional blackmail. He got worse in his teens, but
Reinette refused to seek outside help. I think she had
some sort of idea that to do so would be tantamount to
admitting failure. She would never even admit that anything was wrong, and yet she was the one who suffered
most. She was lined and grey long before she should
have been. As Philip got older, his hang-up manifested
itself in different ways. There were tantrums when he felt
he'd been slighted, public quarrels with his first girl-
friends . . . We were all relieved when he married Rose.
She was about eight years older than him, a strong personality who adored him, but still Philip wasn't happy.
She didn't love him enough, he believed. He resented her
parents, her friends, anyone for whom she felt affection . . .'

'Yes?'

Kemp had paused and Valentine thought his face
looked as if it were carved out of granite.

'There was one thing he did that . . . I just don't know!'
Kemp exclaimed angrily. 'I've been around the world
and seen some terrible things, Valentine, cruelties I
wouldn't want you to know about, but for some reason
this one action of Philip's appalled me, though I've witnessed so much worse in my time. Rose had a cat, a
beautiful, highly pedigreed sealpoint. Philip hated it because Rose loved it—more than she loved him, he
believed. He was quite honestly jealous of a cat! Well,
perhaps that wasn't so unusual, but what he did was . . .
One day he took this delicate and nervous little creature,
who had rarely even been allowed into the garden unless
someone was with her; he put her in his car and took her
out to a stretch of veld in the middle of nowhere, and left
her there.'

'Oh, God!' Valentine's lips curved downwards.

'Then he went home and told Rose what he'd done.
She forced him to show her where he'd dumped the
animal, and the fact that she went back there day after

day, calling and looking for her pet, merely increased Philip's belief that she'd loved the cat more than she did him.'

'Ah, no!' Valentine shook her head and the habitual cautious composure had vanished from her lovely voice in the spontaneity of her sympathy. 'Poor Rose, and the poor little cat ... I hope it didn't suffer too long. And poor, poor Philip!'

Kemp looked at her intently. 'You do pity him after all.'

'Oh, I always have,' she confided slowly and sadly. A gesture of one slender hand was indicative of her helpless frustration. 'He must have been unhappy all his life, a self-inflicted unhappiness. If I'd known——'

'It would have made no difference,' Kemp interrupted tautly.

'None,' she agreed sharply, sensing criticism. 'I couldn't have been blackmailed emotionally.'

'You must have come as a shock to Philip,' Kemp suggested, grimly reflective. 'All his life he had been able to force the love he demanded from people, his parents and wife, and there you were, unmoved and unmoving.'

'A monster of cruelty,' Valentine agreed caustically.

'For God's sake, Valentine!' Kemp exclaimed explosively. 'Your hostile manner does nothing to win you sympathy, you know. Doesn't it help you at all to know this about my cousin?'

She shrugged nonchalantly. 'I suppose it confirms my belief that he was emotionally immature ... unstable. And it seems to suggest that I alone can't have been responsible for the break-up of his marriage——'

'I'm afraid you were, however inadvertently,' Kemp interrupted her harshly. 'You'll know from the evidence that he left Rose only twelve days before he committed suicide.'

For a fleeting moment her dark head drooped, the sunlight catching the rich brown sheen of her curls. Then she stared at him, a brilliant forced smile on her lips.

'Rose must have been crazy,' she said in a hard, tight little voice.

'She loved him,' he contradicted her. 'Whatever he did, she loved him.'

'That's what I said,' she mocked. 'Love makes fools of us all, doesn't it?'

'I doubt if you know much about that particular emotion, sweetheart,' Kemp derided. 'Whom have you ever loved, Valentine?'

'Thank God, I've only the experience of observing what it does to others,' she said.

'Yes?'

He sounded sceptical and Valentine let her gaze slide casually away from his tense, contemptuous face. She stared unseeingly at the clear blue mountains. Dear God, if Kemp knew—She recalled the revenge he had threatened to take on St Valentine's Day, her most miserable birthday to date. He had said he would have her at his feet and in tears; he had sworn to bring down the citadel of her pride. He had wanted her humble to the point of humiliation, he had said.

If he but knew it, though most of the pride was intact, and there had not been a solitary tear, still she was in a sense at his feet, and for as long as she remained in daily contact with him, he would be able to trample over her.

Valentine practised a smile in the direction of the mountains before facing him again.

'Is that today's session of punishment over with, Kemp?' she asked bitingly. 'It is punishment you're aiming at, isn't it, with these constant references to my past?'

'Your past is also your present,' he retorted tersely. 'What happened to Philip is still affecting you now.'

'You're making sure of that, aren't you? Every mention of Philip is meant to torture me——'

'You fool!' Kemp interrupted her furiously. 'Do you think I enjoy talking about Philip? There are a hundred other methods I could use if I wanted to torture you, more enjoyable methods . . . for both of us.'

Valentine looked at him warily and saw his meaning in the intense blue glance which had dropped to her lips and then the open buttons of her shirt.

'No, thank you,' she said tartly.

'You look wildly romantic, sitting in a field of flowers,' he mused. 'The sun is touching your hair and your eyes are the colour of dark sapphires; a woman as lovely as you is like a miracle. Red lips and a skin with the lustre of pearls . . . You're all invitation, a demon and an angel. And those legs, Valli . . . Why not?'

She met his hard smile with one of her own. 'I'm afraid the memory of the last time lives on, Kemp. I haven't forgotten the bruises I collected, still less the impression I gained that I was nothing more than an object to you, that you were using me as you'd use a woman you'd bought.'

'I've never had any need to buy myself a woman, sweetheart,' he told her angrily.

'No, I don't suppose you have,' she said in a considering little voice as cold as snow. 'I can imagine how willingly and how gratefully women grant whatever you demand . . . But I'm different, Kemp.'

'Very, very different,' he confirmed drily. 'Totally unique and unutterably lovely.'

'I don't want you to touch me,' she said very clearly.

But he was already pulling her into his arms, gently but firmly. 'There'll be no bruises this time, I promise you,' He murmured against her loose silken curls. Valentine's eyes were wide and expectant as they encountered the brilliance of his, and her lips were parting already, their redness a provocation.

Kemp kissed her and she felt a warm melting sensation within her. She was boneless, and weightless. She might have been floating. Her hands strayed to his shoulders and then the back of his head, and she moaned in protest at the utter sensuality of his mouth as their lips writhed sinuously together, twining in a message of mutual hunger.

His arms tightened about her as he lowered her gently back on to the grass, and when their mouths came apart they each drew a shuddering breath. Why, why did he have to affect her so powerfully, and so rapidly? Valentine turned her lips back to his and their mouths seemed to merge, symbolising the deeper oneness that she craved with a yearning which would soon become unbearable. Kemp, she vaguely realised, was in control of the situation, with passion kept at bay, the expertise and finesse of his embrace a sure indication of his deep experience.

'Damn you!' she said furiously when her mouth was free again. 'You don't even want me!'

'Make me want you, Valli,' he challenged tautly.

'I will,' she vowed tempestuously.

'The way you want me?'

'Yes!'

He was cruel, her mind protested. This was the torture he had spoken of. Dear God, where were pride and sanity, and the coolness she had cultivated for so long?

He lay next to her, on his side now, waiting for her to act, and Valentine's fingers strayed to the buttons of his soft blue shirt and began to unfasten them, tentatively at first but becoming swifter. Then she pulled herself closer to him, caressing his warm skin, tugging gently at the fine curling hairs on his chest while her mouth pressed lightly against his, her tongue just flickering over his lips as she succeeded, at terrible cost, in concealing her own desperate hunger.

Finally, just when she was coming to the despairing conclusion that here was a man totally immune to her, Kemp moved convulsively, gathering her hard against him and then pushing her on to her back once more, lowering himself on to her.

'God, Valli . . . You're a witch!'

'Casting bad spells over men,' she supplied in a moment of bitterness, remembering suddenly that revenge was all he sought. 'I hate you, Kemp.'

'You want me,' he stated arrogantly, and claimed her mouth.

The rhythms and pulses of their bodies had quickened their tempo and now Valentine realised that Kemp's skin was as heated as hers, and his breathing equally erratic. He drew back a little to deal with the buttons of her shirt, next freeing her breasts from the confinement of her bra and finally unfastening the waistband and zip of her shorts.

'You're so unbelievably beautiful,' he muttered urgently.

His fingers gently teased her nipples into hard, hot points, and Valentine gasped with delight, her hands clutching feverishly at his shoulders.

'Ah . . . God! Kemp, please!'

The agonised appeal in her voice and eyes made him draw a sharp breath and he lowered his head to put his mouth to each thrusting breast in turn, his tongue flicking lightly at the tips, darting over them until throbbing pleasure was almost pain. Above them the sun beamed from a cloudless sky and the mountains reared in serene majesty, but Valentine, groaning with pleasure, knew nothing of them. This man filled her world, became her world, and she was helpless under the welter of passion he aroused in her with even his lightest, most careless touch.

'I want you,' she pleaded frenziedly, half crazed with desire, her flesh burning under his hands which he had slid beneath her, kneading and caressing her back and shoulders with powerful strokes.

Kemp's mouth made a slow, sensual journey back to her hot moist lips once more, the weight of his body pressing her back against the soft grass, and Valentine writhed beneath him, her hands moving convulsively over his damp back, her breasts crushed hard against his chest.

'Valentine!' Her name was a gasping groan on his lips.

'Please,' she screeched, feeling his male hardness against her body and knowing he wanted her as much as she did him.

A high, wild little cry broke from her as he drew back and the sound seemed to hang quivering in the still air, terrible in the longing it conveyed. Now his hands were sliding and gliding erotically over her flat stomach and hips, down to the satiny skin of her thighs, and Valentine trembled violently.

'Kemp! For pity's sake, take me,' she begged shamelessly in a voice that was raw, while her body jerked frantically upward towards his. 'End this torture. Take me!'

He seemed to draw further away from her. 'Ah, yes . . . you see! Just one of the myriad ways in which I can torture you, my lovely Valentine. No! Don't touch me again just now,' he added sharply when she reached for him.

'You're cruel,' she moaned. Their mingled perspiration was acid-sharp on her swollen breasts and every nerve-end, every drop of blood, cried out for his possession.

'Crueller than you know, and cruel to myself too,' he murmured ironically, sitting up and pulling his long ago discarded shirt on again. 'But you see, I think I must be a conventional man: romantic as a field of flowers might be, I prefer lovemaking to reach its conclusion in the comfort of a wide soft bed with all the long dark night ahead of me.'

'You bastard,' Valentine whispered intensely, sitting up and gathering the two halves of her front-fastening bra together over her breasts with shaking hands.

This, then, was what he had meant when he said he could torture her. He was clever. To tempt and then to deny; to take her to the very brink of ecstasy and then abandon her there, was a far greater torment than to have him take loveless possession of her would be. Dear God, he knew her and her needs too well.

'Another reason is that I have an appointment with Emma Ducaine in a short while,' he went on lightly, a half-smile tugging at his lips as he noted the hot blaze of her eyes and the wild tangle of her curls. 'We're taking the horses out.'

At that moment she felt hatred like a pure white flame inside her. 'You can't do this to me!'

'Why not?' he derided as she stood up.

'I won't accept it.' The tremor had gone from her hands as anger gave her strength of mind, and she buttoned her shirt rapidly. 'I won't allow your revenge to take this form, Kemp. I'll——'

'God! You're still far from ready to become my lover,' he said with sudden inexplicable fury. 'You don't even trust me!'

'Why should I? And don't you trust me either in future, Kemp,' she warned with a malicious little smile. She rose gracefully, zipping up her shorts and tucking her shirt into the waistband. With her head flung back she looked at him from very clear eyes. 'I'll seduce you. When you're least expecting it, I'll seduce you.'

'What a threat!' Kemp laughed, relaxing again. 'You're incredible. But why warn me? Now I shall be on my guard.'

'I can, you know,' she threatened gently.

'I shall look forward to your attempt.' He surveyed her proud face thoughtfully. 'You don't accept defeat easily, do you?'

'I refuse to countenance it.'

'I'm afraid you'll have to.' Kemp glanced at his watch. 'I must be getting back. Emma will be arriving shortly. Are you coming back with me or staying here?'

The tip of Valentine's tongue appeared, exploring the rawness of her kiss-swollen lips, and her eyes grew amused. 'It would be too cruel to let her see me return with you, and all my lipstick gone.'

'You look very beautiful even without it . . . more like a woman than the fairytale heroine you so often resemble. In fact, your face tells a very explicit story,' he mocked.

'A story Emma might benefit from knowing if she still hasn't abandoned hope,' Valentine suggested sweetly. She shrugged. 'But it's not my duty to help you let her down gently, Kemp. Go back and do it yourself. I'm staying here.'

'Planning the great seduction scene?' he challenged.

'That's it exactly,' she countered smartly, her smile dazzling.

He shook his head. 'The fantasies women indulge in! A waste of time, but I suppose as it's Sunday you have plenty. I'll see you later, sweetheart.'

'Oh, and don't forget to let Emma know I've been encouraging you to give up her beloved Country Life,' Valentine called after him flippantly.

Kemp looked back, laughing, but the smile faded from Valentine's face as he turned away again.

Harvesting progressed. An air of quiet satisfaction seemed to pervade Fleurmont and its neighbouring estates as the workers became confident that they were going to beat the weather. Once the vintage was *onder dak* it could do what it would. Only Freddie Jansen remained pessimistic.

Valentine watched and waited. Her purpose remained fixed and a certain vibrant anger gave her strength. She did not deserve to be punished for what Philip had done and she was determined to thwart Kemp's cruel tactics. It was the cleverest thing he could have thought of; but then he knew too well the deep needs of her passionate nature and the powerful effect he had on her. She didn't doubt that he intended making love to her again and then leaving her frustrated, probably again and yet again if she remained here.

And she refused to stand for it. She knew she did not merit such treatment and she could almost hate him for believing she did. A fey, reckless mood lay on her these days, adding an air of gypsy wildness to her beauty, and Kemp often looked at her speculatively.

She had meant it when she had threatened to seduce him, and now she was simply biding her time, waiting for the right moment. She had both intelligence and insight enough to recognise the complexity of the man. His moods were many and varied, some of them dark, so that he was broodingly unapproachable, and she knew that just now he was in the grip of frustration at having to be here instead of travelling the world, doing the work that had truly been a vocation with him.

But the right mood would come, she knew, and then— Kemp wouldn't be able to alter the situation. He could desire her at times, and she would make sure he wanted her sufficiently to abandon the intention of merely tempting her. Valentine often smiled to herself as she anticipated her final victory, heedless of what she might be doing to herself when she achieved it. Emotional safety didn't seem to matter any longer in this conflict: triumph was all-important.

'What's going on between you and Kemp?' Salome asked with a grin one morning as she stopped to talk after bringing a set of clean glasses to the visitors' room. 'You watch him and he watches you, and what happens? Precisely nothing. Maude says you're still alone in your own bed when she takes you coffee every morning.'

'You've been interrogating her, Salome,' Valentine teased. 'It isn't automatically a matter of course that propinquity will drive two people into each other's arms.'

'Propinquity?' Salome shook her startling amber head. 'That doesn't sound like what I mean. I'm talking about that . . . that tension between you and him. I had thought that two strong characters like you would . . . But perhaps there's too much strength of will on both sides. That can lead to a clash of personalities according to my magazines. Or perhaps you just believe in marriage?'

'I do, as a matter of fact,' Valentine said coolly.

But marriage was an ideal she had put firmly out of sight by this time. Men married where they loved and respected. Kemp was a man she would have married; she had known that since her first sight of him; her man, but for all that had come between them. Now he despised her and even his desire wasn't enough if he could set out to deliberately frustrate her own.

But she would make it enough, she vowed.

'I think it would be nice if there was a party at Fleurmont after the last grapes are in,' she suggested to Kemp at breakfast one morning.

'As you wish. Just as long as you and Sylvie and Salome handle the arrangements,' he gave his permission easily, watching her face and seeing her smile of satisfaction. 'You love parties, don't you?'

'What woman doesn't?'

'Many women—the plain and the shy, for a start,' he retorted. 'Do you ever think of your less blessed sisters, Valentine?'

'Frequently, wishing I was like them,' she said, borne down for a moment by the curse of the beauty he derided.

'Yet you'd never deliberately subdue your beauty or mute that charm, would you?' he challenged.

'Never,' she agreed with a smile. 'I'd be a hypocrite if I made myself . . . less than I am.'

'And this wish for a party springs from a purely feminine desire to sparkle in your most flattering setting, I imagine,' he mocked. 'Go ahead and enjoy yourself then. Spend as much as you like on catering and music. The account books tell me that the estate is flourishing.'

'And shall I act as hostess?' she enquired lyrically, eyes sparkling with mischief.

'Why should you want that rôle?' His lips twisted. 'Because you know it will upset Emma?'

'Oh, I'd quite forgotten Emma,' Valentine dismissed the girl airily. 'But don't you think, Kemp, that it's my place to be the hostess?'

'Conceivably, it's Sylvie's,' he countered impatiently. 'She's been on Fleurmont longer than you.'

'Ah, but her name hasn't been linked with yours, and you are, after all, the owner,' Valentine reminded him with gentle malice.

'Now what rumours have you been hearing?' he asked, looking amused. 'The same ones that Mrs Ducaine has warned me about?'

'Probably.' She laughed, a sound of sheer delight. 'As

you know, I went out with Gary last night, and he thought he ought to tell me that already it's being whispered that I'm your mistress.'

'I imagine he was very anxious for you to deny it?' Kemp ventured tautly.

'Well, yes, since he regards me as one of his favourite girl-friends,' she confided in a lilting tone that was full of amused pleasure.

He gave her a sharp, assessing look, noting the glimmer of suppressed laughter in her eyes.

'And did you deny it, Valli?' he asked silkily.

The laughter surfaced enchantingly again. 'In an oblique sort of way,' she conceded happily. 'I gave a secretive little smile and told him that you and I were just good friends.'

Kemp laughed with genuine amusement. 'You really are a witch . . . How you manipulate those young idiots!'

'They like it.' Her mirth died suddenly and a hint of the old tragedy turned her mouth bitter. 'Kemp, I don't want you to think I played with Philip in the same way. Innocent as I was then, and ignorant of the extent of my . . . my power, I did at least realise that he was someone who took both himself and life very seriously. I never teased him.'

'Forget Philip,' he advised abruptly. 'Remembering does you a disservice . . . It chases the laughter from your eyes, leaving you looking sad and far more experienced than you actually are.'

Valentine's eyes opened very wide. 'And isn't that what you want?' she asked in a carefully controlled little voice.

'No, my dear, it isn't,' he drawled, pushing back his chair and standing up. 'You've to be at your enticing best, flying all that bright beauty like a banner if you're still intent on the great seduction idea . . . Or have you abandoned it?'

Her smile was a gradual, shatteringly lovely thing. 'No, I haven't,' she assured him in a slow, silvery voice.

'I've been waiting for it,' he told her ironically.

'Somehow the right time and the right place haven't coincided,' she said reflectively, tilting her head to one side as she looked up at him. 'I'm biding my time until you're in an appropriate mood, you see.'

'Your attempt should be a memorable occasion,' he laughed.

'Attempt?' she queried musically. 'Oh, but Kemp, I shall succeed.'

'That I doubt, sweetheart. You see, I can only be seduced when I want to be,' he told her smoothly, his amusement evaporating. 'God, Valentine, haven't you yet realised that, enchantingly lovely though you are, that dark power which is causing you so much bitterness and suffering only extends to a certain type of man . . . A man like Philip. You're probably wise to avoid Henry van Wyk as well, but can you honestly imagine either Gary or Adam throwing their lives away when they finally realise that you don't love them and never will? And even less than them, can you affect me. I would never die for you, Valli. Nor can you seduce me unless I allow you to. Think about it.'

With which warning, he went from the room, leaving Valentine to reflect on his advice, finally coming to the conclusion that he had merely been playing a word-game, trying to deflate her self-confidence.

Both Sylvie Hattingh and Salome Jansen approved of the idea of a party and in the days that followed, the three of them became as busy as the men who were bringing in the grapes, constantly consulting each other. Neither of the women seemed surprised that Valentine should take most of the arrangements upon herself and she was grateful when they left the final authority to her. She had discovered in herself a flair for organising such affairs, knowing exactly what she wanted, and she was determined that Fleurmont's harvest party should be one the entire district would remember and discuss for months to come.

Then, at the end of March, the last of the year's vintage

was brought in on a glittering blue and gold day. They watched the final load, decorated with the autumnal colours of the Cabernet vine's leaves, come in, and there were smiles all round. Even Kemp's frustration at being responsible for all this was sublimated for the moment, Valentine thought as she stood between him and James Hattingh.

'I see you're smiling, Freddie,' James challenged the Coloured man who had joined them.

'*Ja-nee! Die oes is in,*' Freddie conceded pensively in his own language.

'The harvest is in,' Kemp repeated reflectively. 'Another wine year over with.'

'*Ja!*' Freddie's smile disappeared, but he sounded more satisfied with life. 'A celebration, a short time of quiet, and then it all starts again, the pruning, planting and tilling, worrying all the summer, wondering what the next vintage will be like.'

'Man! You're only so pessimistic because Salome is unfailingly cheerful,' James laughed. 'Come on, I can see Binnie and your Trevor getting in everyone's way again.'

As the pair departed, Valentine touched Kemp's arm.

'But you, Kemp?' she asked when he looked at her enquiringly. 'All that long process Freddie mentioned; will you be here for it?'

'I don't know, Valentine,' he said expressionlessly, shaking his head, and the sun on his hair made it seem almost fair. 'I haven't decided yet.'

'What's causing the delay?' she ventured quietly. 'You're a decisive man, usually, aren't you?'

'There's no immediate need for a decision.' He smiled derisively. 'Were you thinking of offering me advice?'

'I wouldn't dream of it,' she denied haughtily. A smile flashed out. 'Well, I suppose I might, I have in fact, but I would never expect you to be influenced by anyone's recommendations, Kemp. In the end, you'll always do exactly what you want to do.'

'You'd do well to remember that,' he said bitingly, but she laughed, shaking her head.

He was warning her not to anticipate victory, she knew, but her purpose remained fixed.

Smiling, Valentine returned to the house. Another wine year was ended and the young wines would be racked and filtered in the cellars, ready for the vital tastings. Tonight the workers would hold their own noisy celebrations, financed by the estate, down at their quarters, while she—she had her own party to prepare for.

Because it was her own, she reflected, a present she was giving to herself, something she would be able to recall with pleasure one day when she looked back on this time of pain.

It was her party and she was going to be the star. She looked at the sky happily. She had made alternative arrangements lest the weather change, but it had remained clear and it was going to be a hot night, probably one of the last that season, so the party would be outside.

Later in the evening she set about dressing and making up for the star's rôle, and for once in her life she was ready at the time she had meant to be.

The hostess, she had come to the decision, ought to be tastefully dressed, so the dress she had chosen was less outrageous than many of hers, and without a flounce to be seen, but as well as being elegant it was infinitely seductive, its fit revealing every tender line and curve of her young body. Of midnight blue taffeta, it was pencil-slim and strapless, and slit to near the top of one thigh. Her high-heeled sandals were strappy creations of criss-crossed silver and gold, and about her throat and one upper arm she clasped snake-like strands of entwined silver and gold, and similar strands were visible among her shining dark curls.

Luxuriously perfumed and exotically made up, Valentine put a smile on her face and went to enjoy her party.

CHAPTER EIGHT

'Are you and Kemp by any chance announcing your engagement tonight?' James Hattingh asked Valentine as they whirled among the other pairs of dancers.

'No, I'm afraid not,' Valentine replied with a smile that was both radiant and mischievous.

'Not yet? Sylvie was saying only the other day how perfectly matched you are.'

Valentine lowered her eyes demurely. Regret filled her. She and Kemp could have made a perfect match, if only . . . But how many people down through the ages had brought out, and with what poignant truth, that saw about those last two words being the saddest of all? For there still burnt like some perpetual flame within her, the unfaltering knowledge that Kemp was the right man for her.

The Hattinghs were not alone in their assumption of a relationship between her and Kemp. Several people who had spoken to her tonight had coupled them, so obviously his essential rightness for her was evident to them as well. Valentine knew she was compounding the erroneous rumours by not swiftly denying them, but she hadn't been able to bring herself to disabuse them of the idea that she and Kemp were a pair. She derived a curious, bitter-sweet pleasure from being linked with him, however mistakenly, as if all these people were confirming that moment of recognition her very first sight of him had brought.

Only Emma Ducaine failed to see them as a well-matched pair, or perhaps she did subconsciously do so, and that was why she was fighting so hard.

Valentine looked for the girl, saw her dancing with Kemp once more, and felt a pang of compassion. Tonight Emma had plainly sought to adopt her rival's style, for her soft spring green dress bore the characteristically elaborate frills and flounces of the style Valentine had made her own and then eschewed tonight. Unfortunately, while a pretty girl, Emma lacked Valentine's height and slenderness, and would have suited something simpler. Her personality, too, lacked the essential frivolity which was complemented by such frothy creations.

The party was a perfect one. Valentine smiled complacently as James relinquished her to an insistent Adam and went to join Sylvie. Perfect, and all hers. Kemp had told her to spend as much as she wished and his generosity had freed her to demand only the best, although she was wise enough not to equate quality with expensiveness. The catering firm was the best she had been able to find, the band was a well-known one from Cape Town and the outdoor decorations and lighting were exquisite. The guests were clearly enjoying themselves and they made a beautiful sight, especially those who danced. The women were a joy to look at, she thought, in their myriad colours. It was as if a host of exotic flowers bloomed in the garden just for this one night.

And at the centre of them, the lure to which everyone's eyes kept returning, was Valentine herself. She was fey tonight; strength and purpose and a hint of mischievous delight gave her a light that shone from within, and James had not been alone in assuming that this must be a special occasion for her. She drifted past their startled eyes, shimmering with loveliness. Queen for a night, she was utterly sure of herself, and her wondrous smiles were breathtaking while her eyes sparkled like jewels at one moment and glowed luminously the next. Her partners gave her little rest, for Adam, Gary and Desmond, and others as well, were all there, anxious to be seen within that aura of sheer magic which surrounded her. She was a creature from the realms of faerie, an effortless fantasy combining pure wild romance with a certain dark glowing power whose mystery made the intelligent fear for her.

Kemp was one who saw it. 'Such unmatched loveliness must surely mean you're doomed, my poor Valli,' he taunted gently when he danced with her.

'Not if I can help it,' she murmured.

'The men are all in despair . . . and the women despairing in a wholly different way,' he went on mockingly.

'I don't believe you. They're all enjoying themselves.'

'And enjoying watching you enjoying yourself. It gives people great pleasure to look at you, and the artifice and trouble that go into enhancing your natural beauty would suggest that you take your responsibility seriously.'

'My responsibility . . . is to give pleasure?' she queried thoughtfully.

'You're richly blessed,' he told her with a slight smile.

'And cursed. You know that.'

'There's usually an antidote to curses.'

'Ah, yes, but that's in the fairy stories,' she reminded him whimsically. 'A quest fulfilled, and the curse is lifted.'

'And aren't you straight out of a fairytale?' he derided.

Her smile was ravishing. 'No. I'm quite simply—a woman,' she told him liltingly.

'And glorying in it.' He paused. 'I've noticed how very infrequently you refer to yourself as a girl as most of your sex and age would do. Yet there's so much missing from you as a woman. You're not a whole woman by any means. You never cry, for a start.'

Her bright lips puckered in mock disappointment. 'Incomplete. Aren't you proud of me then, Kemp?'

'You're a born flirt,' he informed her in a derogatory tone. 'But tonight . . . you're perfect. As perfect as one of the stars up there. Yet a dark star, I rather think.'

'You make me sound . . . I'm not evil, Kemp,' she protested, serious for a moment.

'Not in yourself, no,' he conceded grimly. 'It's that

doom I mentioned. You could be the catalyst to great tragedy so very easily.'

'Could—and have been! Is that what you're saying?' she asked sharply, stiffening.

'Ah, no, Valentine!' he said resignedly. 'Don't let your enjoyment be marred. Tonight is for pleasure.'

Yet he it was who had brought forth the jarring reminder of her past. Deliberately? Why not, when he despised her? Revenge was all that interested him. Dear God, if only there was not this past tragedy lying between them like a great impenetrable wall——

Dancing with him was a sweetness to break her mind. A deep throbbing awareness made her lethargic so that she was doing little more than swaying in his arms. Her eyelids, coloured with a dark frosted blue, felt heavy, and they dropped, languidly, over her eyes.

'Valentine?' Kemp's lips were close to her temple.

'Do you remember that time we danced together at that restaurant in Stellenbosch, Kemp?' she asked dreamily, with a little break in her voice. 'On my birthday.'

'Forget that,' he adjured harshly.

Her lashes fluttered upwards to reveal to his hard gaze the languor in her sapphire eyes.

'I just wanted to say—this makes up for that,' she told him with a little smile. 'I like dancing with you ... this way.'

He laughed, drawing her closer but still holding her lightly, and her desire became an intolerable weight. Her limbs were heavy with it and there was a fiercely pounding ache deep within her, a hunger she would not allow him to callously frustrate again.

He seemed to know how close she was coming to putting her sworn plan into action because, as they drew apart when the music stopped, she saw that his expression was very hard. 'Vintage Valentine,' he praised cruelly. 'All seduction. Your tactics are worthy of the greatest courtesan and with anyone but me, my dear, they'd undoubtedly be successful. But keep it up. I'm enjoying the spectacle.'

'I hate you,' she said in a level voice, smiling brilliantly because people were watching them.

With anyone but him, he had said. Valentine turned away, wondering for the first time if perhaps victory was going to be harder to achieve than she had confidently imagined. With anyone but him . . . Because Kemp still hated her on Philip's behalf. Obviously.

A little later, going to her bedroom to renew her lipstick, Valentine knew Emma had spotted her and was following. She sighed. Tonight was not a time for confrontations, but if Emma was determined to speak to her there was little she could do to avoid it.

She was already seated at her dressing-table when Emma appeared in the doorway.

'I want to speak to you, Valentine.'

'I gathered that.' Valentine sorted through the various lipsticks in her large partitioned make-up box. 'Yes?'

Emma came further into the room. 'I'm appealing to you,' she began resolutely.

'To my better nature?'

'If you like.' Emma was very earnest, pleading. 'Leave Kemp alone, Valentine.'

'Why?' Valentine found the lipstick she wanted and took the top off, concentrating on her own reflection although Emma's image had appeared in the mirror as well.

'Because he'll never take his proper place among us with a woman like you. You're preventing his . . . his becoming one of us.'

Valentine shook her head slightly. 'He'll never truly belong to this milieu, Emma, but that has nothing to do with me,' she said quietly. 'Can't you see the truth of that? Kemp Irvine will never be a member of any group of people. He's one, alone . . . Think of the eagle, soaring in freedom. The rest of us are like butterflies, fluttering close to the earth.'

'Yourself included?' Emma asked curiously, and hope had entered her voice.

But Valentine lifted her head with all the arrogance of truly self-aware beauty and power, saying, 'I could soar with him.'

If he would only let her, the bleak thought followed.

'But why should you have him?' Helpless tears had sprung into the other girl's eyes as she recognized something far beyond her ability to contest. 'I'm in love with him. But you, Valentine . . . Why Kemp? Please . . . You could have any man you want!'

'Suppose that it's Kemp I want? What then, Emma?' Valentine enquired coolly. Satisfied with the bright smoothness of her lips, she closed the tube of lipstick and turned to look at the girl. She continued more gently, 'You're being very silly, you know. If you want a man, you set out to work on him, win him, with your own worth. Attacking your rivals can serve no purpose.'

'I hate you—I despise you!' Emma exclaimed tempestuously, angry frustrated tears overflowing as she retreated. 'And I know this, Valentine McLaren—so does Kemp. He might make you his mistress, but he'll never marry you. He'll never forget what you did to Philip de Villiers.'

She whirled out of the room and Valentine heard the rush of her feet as she departed—probably seeking one of the bathrooms in which to cry out all her lovesick jealousy, Valentine guessed sympathetically.

She turned back to her reflection once more. A shadow seemed to lie in the depths of her sapphire eyes. Emma was so wrong in most of what she thought she knew of Kemp, having invested his enigma with the ideal personality she wanted him to have, but she had been correct, horribly correct, in that last statement she had flung at her. Kemp would never forget—or forgive—what had happened to his cousin.

Later that night Kemp and Valentine were to be seen dancing together again. The band had cleverly reserved all their most romantic tunes for the latter half of the party, by which time any inhibitions would have dissolved in the prevailing spirit of conviviality and new friendships had been formed.

Kemp held her very close, but Valentine wished they could be closer. She was slender and graceful in his arms, a miraculous composition of regality and yielding femininity, her pale shoulders gleaming like silk, the midnight darkness of her hair a perfumed mystery of curls. She was quivering, so slightly that it was imperceptible to everyone save the man who touched her.

It was strange, she reflected: he induced this physical weakness in her yet at the same time he strengthened her. She knew she was the star of the night, but knew too that his presence was partly responsible. Without it, she might not have sparkled quite so brilliantly or born herself with quite such self-assurance. He challenged her, yet simultaneously provided her with the strength to meet that challenge.

Her long dark eyelashes swept upwards to reveal the soft lambency of her eyes, and she discovered that Kemp was smiling ironically.

'What's amusing you?' she asked.

He laughed softly. 'I was just thinking how much I'd like to dance a good old-fashioned tango with you ... An elegant and wonderfully sensual dance, sweetheart.'

A delicately provocative smile touched the feminine red mouth.

'We make an ideal couple, don't we?' she challenged mischievously.

'Oh, perfect,' he drawled. 'Everyone else seems to think so too.'

'Ah, yes.' Delighted, suppressed laughter gave her voice a shivery sound. 'I too have been made aware of the prevailing trend of thought. James even asked me if we were announcing our engagement tonight, and said it would be a perfect match!'

'Can you be trying to inveigle me into a proposal of marriage?' Kemp taunted.

'I've never been stupid. No, I'm merely trying to disconcert you,' she confessed demurely. 'Nothing seems to shock you.'

'Nevertheless, the fact that public opinion has taken us to such a respectable stage is faintly surprising,' he conceded. 'As ideal as we may appear together . . .'

His tone was very pointed and clearly he felt it unnecessary to finish the sentence. Valentine's smile grew bitter.

'I know,' she agreed tartly. 'I know the things you feel for me, Kemp, things like contempt and hatred, all adding up to a wish for revenge. But just for tonight, couldn't you yield a little . . . show me some kindness?'

'Kindness is the last thing I want to show you, Valentine,' he stated harshly.

Her eyes widened. 'You're just like me: you won't even bend.'

'Oh, I can bend when it suits me to do so. I just can't be bent. There's a difference,' he told her silkily.

'You're warning me, aren't you?' Valentine queried.

'Clever girl,' he approved derisively. 'Yes, and I hope you are also clever enough to heed it. You're a wonderful witch and I'm deriving enormous entertainment from your performance but, ultimately, all you'll be inviting is your own humiliation.'

'We shall see,' she threatened steadily.

'You have to be a masochist!' Kemp exploded furiously. 'You claim to know me, so haven't you yet realised that I can't be manipulated . . . that I won't be? I resent the attempt. You alienate yourself entirely from sympathy and all you'll receive in the end is yet another rejection. Why set yourself up this way?'

'No, no, I've set you up,' she corrected him wickedly.

His smile was a distorted mockery and his blue eyes blazed with anger. 'As you just said, we shall see.'

Valentine knew that if she succeeded in seducing him,

Kemp's hatred would be intensified, but she no longer cared. Since he hated her anyway ... Her inherent instinct for emotional self-preservation had long since been swallowed up by the strength of her resentment. He could not, must not, be allowed to get away with his rejection of her that day when he had made love to her under the mountains in a field full of flowers and then turned from her, mocking her frustration. It had been meant as part of his revenge for Philip, and she hadn't deserved it.

Kemp was often with her during those last hours of the party, dancing with her or keeping her beside him as they mingled with the guests, his anger either abated or under control, and Valentine continued to enjoy herself.

The catering firm had discreetly removed all traces of their presence, and the band departed at the hour that had been agreed on. Some of their guests had departed, the older ones, those who had to work in the morning, those who had babysitters to free from duty, but those without responsibilities lingered, many with energy enough left to continue dancing to music which now came from the stereo set, the speakers of which had been moved close to the sitting-room windows.

Much later, however, they too departed, but not before being revived for the drive home with a delightful snack of scrambled ostrich eggs which Salome arrived to cook, and a choice of champagne or coffee.

'Where are the dogs?' Kemp asked idly as he and Valentine strolled towards the house when the last car had driven away.

'They went off with Salome when she returned to bed.'

He glanced towards the east where a pallid light was diluting the blackness. 'I think a lot of people are going to sleep until lunchtime today.'

'They enjoyed it,' she said with smiling pride as they entered the hall.

'Yes. You made it a perfect party, Valentine.' Kemp turned from closing the front door. 'Thank you.'

'And thank you.' She took a step towards him.

Smiling, he shook his head. 'I'm going to bed now, and I too am going to sleep until midday.'

Silently, wondering how to bring about the situation she needed, Valentine turned down the passage beside him. At the door of her bedroom he paused.

'Sleep well, Valentine,' he said.

Valentine switched on the light and turned back to him. 'And you, Kemp?' she asked lightly. 'Did you personally enjoy yourself?'

'Yes, thank you,' he replied urbanely.

A smile flashed. 'It was fun, wasn't it?'

'And you're not in the least tired, are you?' he guessed, looking at her assessingly.

'No. In fact, I feel . . . oh, euphoric, lightheaded!'

A laughing sigh came from her as she lifted her slim arms, the backs of her slender hands coming together high above her tipped-back head. She stood posed like that for a few seconds, tall and straight, the line of her arms as beautifully flowing as any ballerina's, her long fingers fluttering slightly.

'Kemp?'

Slowly she lowered her arms, to rest her hands on his shoulders, feeling the warmth of his skin through his thin shirt. Her red lips were parted and the tip of her tongue appeared tantalisingly while real stars sparkled in her eyes.

Kemp's face was hard.

'So, Valli?' he derided. 'Love-goddess . . . or just an ordinary tart?'

'Find out,' she suggested softly, moving closer to him.

'I don't need to,' he told her sardonically.

Closer she moved, and still closer, until her body was lightly pressed against his. Her hands moved on his shoulders and she offered him her lips silently, striving to control the excitement that was gripping her.

Kemp's lips brushed teasingly across hers. 'Forget it, sweetheart,' he advised shortly.

'Kiss me properly,' she urged fiercely, winding her arms

about him, her cool fingers stroking the back of his neck, then moving up to his thick clean hair.

'You're making a fool of yourself, Valli,' he warned amusedly.

'Properly!'

She closed her eyes because his smile was cruel. She felt his lips touch hers again, hovering lightly, until, finally, his mouth claimed hers completely. Valentine's arms tightened about his neck and she felt Kemp's hands at her waist, steadying her suddenly rocking body.

'Again,' she prompted huskily when the kiss ended.

And he did kiss her again—and again. The long sharing of passion was arousing her to an intolerable pitch of desire. She felt his hands move up her back, to where the skin was bare, and she trembled violently, held fast against him. Her hips began to rotate against him in slow, seductive rhythm and she felt the urgent stirring between his thighs as his lips left hers and he bent his head to press them to the perfumed smoothness of her bare shoulder.

'Have you changed your mind yet?' he mocked, but his voice had roughened.

'No.' She was smiling, angelically alluring, when he looked into her face. 'Make love to me, Kemp.'

'What next then, Valli?' he asked with a sort of contained anger.

His arms had slackened and she stepped back a pace, regarding him with a faint stirring of uncertainty, her lips quivering a little.

'Help me,' she whispered.

His lips twisted. 'Oh no, my beautiful witch,' he denied silkily. 'You're supposed to be seducing me, so go ahead and do it.'

Frustration was a hot hardness in her breast and a tightness in her throat, but his contempt only strengthened her determination. Leaving his arms with a gracefully sinuous twist of her lithe body, she walked the few steps to her bed and turned to face him again. He was still standing in the doorway.

'You want me . . . I know you do,' she challenged.

Her eyes were dark and burning as they held his, her lips a bright sensuous invitation. Slowly, her eyes never leaving his, she twisted her arms round behind her and carefully unzipped her dress. With a soft slither of sound it fell from her body and she was revealed to his gaze, the flawless perfection of her body, the proud firmness of young breasts and the amazing slenderness of her waist.

Kemp's eyes narrowed and his face seemed to tighten, the tanned skin stretched tautly across the beautiful bone-structure.

'A born temptress, both dangerous and delightful,' he commented, apparently idly, but Valentine's eyes sought the outline of his hard male arousal.

'Kemp . . .' There was sorcery in the way she said his name.

He crossed to her then and within seconds they were lying together on the bed while his hands touched, caressed and held, and heat gathered in those sensitive regions of her body that he discovered so quickly.

'God! Valli . . .' His voice was a hoarse gasp, nothing more.

'I want you,' she moaned, completely out of control, aching to know him in her, desire a pulsating, un-restrained hunger.

His mouth touched her breasts and she moaned again at the sensations evoked by the swift stroking of his tongue, stimulating her nipples.

'Kemp . . . Kemp!' His name kept coming from her, uttered in a strange, breaking voice as she clung desperately, as if he were the source of her very life. 'Quickly . . .'

'Valentine!' he groaned in agony.

She felt congested with desire, her body racked by passion, causing her hips to strain forward. When he withdrew from her clinging arms to stand up, she thought it was to remove his own clothes, but after a moment she opened her eyes to see him standing beside the bed, a half-smile playing about his lips as he looked down at the glowing loveliness of her body which was sprawled on the bed in an attitude of wild, expectant abandon.

'Enough, Valentine,' he said quietly.

'No!' It was a cry of despair.

'But yes, sweetheart.' His voice was level, and infinitely cold. 'I won't be one of your victims. I did warn you that I can't be manipulated.'

'Oh, God,' she said in a flat voice, sitting up, drawing her legs up and encircling them with her arms, resting her head on her knees. 'Why do you have to be so strong . . . and I so weak?'

She had not felt tired before, but now she did so, deathly tired, drained and defeated.

'That difference between us is very significant, but I'll leave you to work it out for yourself,' Kemp told her distantly. She heard him sigh slightly. 'Never mind, Valli, it was a performance worthy of an Oscar from first to last. Right from the beginning of the party you rarely faltered.'

'Don't!'

She had flung her head up sharply. The colour of shame still flushed her cheeks, but her mouth was curved bitterly and in her eyes was an expression of dignity which had an odd pathos.

'So, Kemp,' she breathed reflectively. 'Once again you've succeeded in humiliating me.'

'Don't regard it in that light,' he advised her. 'You did your best and suffered an honourable defeat.'

'Don't—don't—don't pity me!' Valentine exclaimed furiously.

His lips quirked. 'I, pity you? You know better than that.'

'Of course,' she agreed acidly, collecting herself. 'I was forgetting what little reason you have to feel anything like pity for me.'

His face grew closed. 'You never learn, do you?' he said disgustedly.

'No. I appear to be quite stunningly stupid, in fact,' she agreed, her voice sharpened by bitterness. 'I really am a fool. I quite honestly thought I could ... seduce you, Kemp. I forgot or disregarded the fact that your strongest desire, where I'm concerned, will always be to either hurt or humiliate me.'

'As I say, you never learn,' he repeated. 'Stop this, Valentine. Bitterness doesn't become you.'

She forced a smile. 'I'm so disappointed in myself, you see,' she mocked, flaying herself. 'I've always prided myself on my intelligence and now it seems to have deserted me. I have only myself to blame, haven't I?'

'Since I did warn you, yes, you have,' he confirmed abruptly. 'But what's the point of self-recrimination? It isn't you, my dear, and it will achieve nothing. What happened to all that pride ... and all that wonderful acting ability?'

'Crushed,' she confessed tartly.

'I don't believe it.' For a moment a smile appeared in his eyes. 'Temporarily absent, perhaps, and not surprising at this uncivilised hour. So you've been defeated, Valentine ... So what? It isn't the end of the world, is it? You'll survive. You can survive anything.'

'I'm sure that's one of the reasons behind your wish to punish me,' she suggested stiffly. 'I'm a survivor, Philip wasn't.'

He turned away from the bed then. 'I believe I've said this to you before—you're punishing yourself.'

'Then why must you add to that punishment?' she flung at his back.

He paused, glancing back at her. 'Do you really think that's what I'm doing? Think about it, and when your intelligence returns to you, we'll discuss it. Meanwhile, get some sleep.'

The door closed quietly behind him and Valentine shivered, realising for the first time in several minutes that she had very little on. How had Kemp managed to remain fully clothed? She reflected tiredly that the fact that he

had was a sure indication of the yawning difference between the intensity of her need for him and what very
little desire he felt for her. And it must very little indeed.

Later, trying to sleep, irritated by the sound of birdsong
outside, she cursed her folly yet again. She had been
stupid, stupid.

Of course Kemp was stronger than her, quite apart
from the fact that the memory of Philip would enable
him to resist her quite easily.

How could she have forgotten that, when she had made
up her mind to seduce him? It was that very strength
which she had known must exist in a man for her to be
able to love him, that she had recognized in Kemp right
at the beginning, before they had even spoken to each
other. To begin with, she had worshipped it in him. She
remembered how she had thought, on the occasion of their
first meeting, that here was a man whom she could never
bring to his knees.

Of course he was stronger than she was. She had been
stupid to forget it. It was the difference between him and
all the other men she had ever known. How otherwise
could she have loved him, but for that invincibility, that
sure inability to be broken or bent by anyone or anything
in life? And she did love him, consumingly, achingly and
despairingly. She loved him with a terrible devouring
force that might have frightened her save that she had
known since about the age of sixteen that she would one
day be capable of such passionate loving.

Kemp had called her a survivor, and when she awoke
from the sleep that eventually claimed her, Valentine's
own belief in that truth was once more unwavering. She
was a survivor and she was not a coward. Thus, she was
not going to leave Fleurmont and her job simply in an
attempt to escape further suffering. To do so would in a
sense be conceding the final victory to Kemp. Anyway, the
idea of going and seeing no more of him was unbearable.

Nevertheless, although Valentine was determined to
endure whatever further humiliations he devised for her,

as she had no doubt he would, she also made up her mind that she would not again provoke him in any way whatsoever. She must never seek him out and arouse his momentary anger because she could never be victorious in any exchange with him. If he wanted revenge for Philip, then he must come to her, unprovoked, and she would endure with as much insouciance as her pride could summon up.

To this end, while not actually avoiding Kemp, Valentine saw less of him than previously, in those still warm April days that followed. She began a whirl of hedonistic activity. There were Adam and Gary and others who asked her out and she was absent from Fleurmont nearly every evening, going to more parties, or to restaurants and hotels, especially those where there was dancing, functions at the university in Stellenbosch when visiting speakers came to deliver speeches, or to shows given by the students covering all the various performing arts. Survival lay in filling one's life and keeping as active as possible, so there was the polo club at weekends, and once she and Adam drove to Cape Town where they went up Table Mountain in the cable car and walked for over an hour, admiring the various views and the enchanting brown dassies basking on the rocks on the sunny side of the mountain, lunching later at Hout Bay on the Atlantic side of the peninsula and ending up at a café near Bloubergstrand in the evening.

'Too many late nights?' Kemp enquired one morning when Valentine entered the breakfast room just as he was finishing his own meal.

'A new hairstyle always makes me late.'

He glanced at the smooth chignon which drew the hair back to reveal every aspect of her exquisite facial bones.

'It suits you,' he said with a faint smile.

'Thank you.'

She thought anguishedly—why did he have to be so . . . so civilized? It was another of the qualities she worshipped in him. Never once, since the party, had he referred to her attempt to seduce him and her subsequent humiliation. It was as if it had never occurred.

'Where did you go last night?' he asked with idle interest as she sipped her coffee.

'Desmond took me to a party at one of the students'
residences at the university.'

Kemp looked at her thoughtfully. 'I've recently heard,
in a somewhat roundabout way, that a lecturer in Lit.
from the Afrikaans faculty has been making regular trips
to Cape Town, seeing Rose de Villiers. I hope it works
out for her. She used to lecture as well. I wonder if she
ever comes up to Stellenbosch.'

'Yes.'

No one else would have noticed the slight tensing of the
fingers curled round the handle of her cup, or the tightening of her facial muscles. Kemp did, however, and his
eyes narrowed.

'What is it?' he queried softly.

'Need you ask?' she retorted, smiling wryly at his ability
to observe the slightest shift of mood in her. 'Rose de
Villiers . . . just another reminder of Philip!'

'It wasn't meant that way,' he said tautly. 'I was
making idle conversation, Valentine. About Rose, not
Philip. You never met her, did you?'

'No, thank God. She didn't attend the inquest. They
said she'd suffered some sort of nervous collapse and was
heavily sedated. I hope I never do. I can face most things,
Kemp, but not that.' Her eyes had darkened and the mask
momentarily fallen away. 'I don't think I behaved
wrongly or irresponsibly with Philip, considering I was
ignorant of both his nature and the fact of his marriage,
but I suppose I must feel some degree of guilt if I can feel
this way about Rose. I wasn't culpable, but I was to
blame—unwittingly.'

'Forget it, Valentine,' Kemp ordered savagely, while
his glance measured the extent of her shame and bitterness. 'You're unlikely to come face to face with Rose.
Coincidence has paid you more than your fair share of
attention already.'

CHAPTER NINE

VALENTINE disliked the cabaret and she objected to some strange singer singling her out with his eyes and serenading her. It was an invasion of privacy.

'Let's go, Adam,' she requested with her most appealing smile. 'I'm not in the mood for this.'

'Is there anything special you'd like to do, anywhere else you'd like to go?' he asked a few minutes later when they were in his car.

'Have I ruined the evening for you?' she asked with charming contrition.

'Of course not,' he denied gallantly. 'Normally your stamina and enjoyment of an evening out is phenomenal, so I can't complain when for once you behave out of character.'

'What a nicely brought up young man you are,' she said with a faint smile. 'I'm sorry, Adam. All I feel like doing is going home. That singer upset me.'

'He had a nerve, I must say, but you can hardly blame him for noticing you,' Adam said as he started the car. 'You're very eye-catching, Valentine. Decorative is the word. And I do wish you'd stop complimenting me on my good manners. It makes me feel I have to behave better than I want to.'

'That's the whole idea,' she laughed.

Adam sighed. 'It's very effective. I've never met anyone so skilled at keeping a man at arm's length!'

He didn't stay at arm's length when they arrived at Fleurmont a while later, but a brief goodnight kiss was all Valentine allowed him after telling him she wasn't going to ask him in.

'Do you keep the same space around yourself where Kemp Irvine is concerned, honey?' he asked as she withdrew.

'Kemp Irvine?'

'Just what is the relationship between the two of you?' Adam probed. 'It was evident to everyone at that harvest party that there was a relationship of some sort.'

Valentine shrugged. 'Perhaps everyone was mistaken,' she said lightly. 'If Kemp and I . . . Would I be going out with you, and the others, Adam? And Kemp sees Emma.'

'You might be broadminded and have . . . What's the phrase? An open relationship?'

Valentine laughed. 'If things were as you suggest between me and Kemp, I wouldn't share him with Emma and I'd hope he wouldn't want to share me with anyone. Goodnight again, Adam, and thank you.'

The sound of his car died away while she was making a fuss of the dogs, and then she went inside. The flickering light from the sitting-room told her the television was on for the late news, but the sound was turned right down and when she looked in, Kemp was in fact reading.

'I'm back,' she said rather obviously, and he looked up enquiringly.

'You're early. Did you have a pleasant evening?' he asked indifferently.

'Oh, reasonable. And you?' Why were they being so polite? 'Did you go out?'

'Yes. I had dinner with the Hattinghs,' he told her, looking at his book again. 'Actually, they appeared to have been expecting you as well.'

'This is the first I've heard of it,' Valentine said casually.

'People assume a lot.'

'Don't they?' She remembered Adam's interrogation. 'You could have corrected the assumption by taking Emma with you.'

He didn't reply to that, but he did look at her again, a faintly exasperated look, as she stood in the doorway, tall and slender in a brief, graceful garment of sapphire-blue silk chiffon, with her dark curls spilling about her slender neck in glorious profusion.

Valentine lifted a graceful shoulder. 'Oh, well, I'm going to bed. Goodnight, Kemp.'

'Goodnight, Valentine.'

She went along to her bedroom, switching the light on as she entered. As always, her eyes sought her reflection in the dressing-table mirror. For a moment she didn't really believe she was seeing what she did, so unexpected was it. Then——

'No!'

The cry of protest was torn from her. Someone had taken up the reddest of her lipsticks and written crudely on the mirror—Remember Philip. It was shocking mainly because she was totally unprepared for it, but it also succeeded in making her obey its simple command. She remembered Philip, and she remembered the hatred felt by those who had been close to him. A moan of anguish came from her as she backed away, still staring at the ugly message as if mesmerized by it.

Kemp's arrival broke her trance. 'What's the matter? Why did you——' he broke off as he saw her face, her eyes almost black in the midst of its whiteness. 'Valentine! What's frightening you?'

She gestured wildly. His eyes went to the mirror and he drew a sharp breath.

'My God!' He put a hand on her shoulder, steadying her because she was swaying.

'How . . . why?' She stopped, swallowing hard and striving desperately for control. The smile she managed was a travesty. 'An unnecessary injunction. I never forget—I'm not permitted to.'

Kemp's eyes narrowed and his hand tightened on her shoulder.

'Just who are you blaming for that piece of . . . cruel juvenility?'

'I'm sorry, I'm sorry!' Valentine gasped as sanity reasserted itself. 'I must have gone mad for a moment. It wouldn't be your way, Kemp . . . But then who?'

'Come away from this place, Valentine.'

His arm was still across her shoulders and she allowed him to lead her back to the sitting-room.

'Do ... do you think I deserve that?' she asked suddenly, as if the answer was the most important thing in the world.

He saw the way her lip was quivering and his arm tightened. 'Don't be ridiculous!'

Just for a moment she turned her face against him, briefly letting him support her weight, the first time she had ever leaned against anyone in need. Then she straightened, her mouth tightening, and went to sit in a chair.

Kemp brought her a drink. She tasted it and set the glass down. 'I'm not going to faint, you know.'

'You're still pale,' he remarked, looking at her intently.

She tried to make her shrug casual. 'I'm sorry. Once again I'm making a fool of myself, but I ... I was frightened, you see. It shocked me.'

He shook his head. 'That's understandable. Stay here, Valentine. I'm going to remove that ... that evil from the mirror.'

Her mind was blank as she waited in the quiet room. He had switched off the television and only a couple of shaded wall lights were on. Above the fireplace the carriage clock ticked rhythmically and she fitted the words to the sound. Remember Philip. Remember ...

Kemp's return startled her.

'Are you all right?'

'Of course.' She tried very hard to smile, but there was a bleak bitterness in her eyes and her face was still paper-white.

Kemp sighed, going across to the dimmer switch and turning the lights up a little. 'You're trying too hard, my dear.'

'Should I let such ... such crudity bring me down?' Her voice wobbled and she compressed her lips hastily. 'There's really nothing to be said, is there?'

'Except to wonder who was responsible.' He stood in front of her, looking grim.

Valentine looked up at him. 'Well . . . who?' she asked slowly. 'I can't believe anyone at Fleurmont could be the perpetrator.'

'Neither can I,' Kemp agreed. As if he was tired, he moved his shoulders, flexing the muscles and then relaxing again. 'Listen, Valentine. When I was with the Hattinghs we heard a car pass, but I just assumed Adam was bringing you home early, especially as we heard it again a short time later, returning in the direction of the public road. Salome would still have been about at that time. Will you wait here for me while I go to her quarters and ask who it was that called?'

'Yes.'

He seemed to hesitate, before leaving the room again.

Valentine heard him go outside and the dogs gave him a noisy welcome which he hushed impatiently. Then there was silence for a time. With no one to witness her, there was no need to keep up appearances and Valentine leaned forward with her elbows on her knees, her face in her hands. This was pure self-pity and she was a fool to indulge in it, but she had never felt so unloved and alone. It was a cold, empty feeling.

She heard Rufus whine excitedly and sat up straight, composing her features. She was a weak and foolish woman to let something so petty distress her so deeply. She had endured worse than this. Already a suspicion of her persecutor's identity was beginning to form and she told herself she should be feeling only compassion.

Kemp re-entered the room and she searched his face, noting the hardness of his brilliant eyes and the disgusted twist of his lips. He sat down opposite her.

'Salome says Emma Ducaine called earlier this evening,' he told her abruptly. 'She wanted to see me, apparently, and I'd forgotten to tell Salome where I was going. My car would have been out of sight when she passed the Hattinghs' house—otherwise she might have joined me there, I suppose, instead of doing what she did. Salome said she went to the bathroom before leaving again ... She'd have known you were safely out of the way since it was her brother you were out with.'

Valentine nodded slightly. 'Yes.'

'You're not surprised, are you?'

'No, are you?'

'I suppose not,' Kemp conceded tautly.

A faint, mocking smile crossed Valentine's pale face. 'Are you sure she hasn't left the same message in your room, Kemp? Because I think she'd very much like you to keep remembering what I did to your cousin.'

'No, I've been in there since coming home,' he said tersely.

'Poor Emma!'

'Is that all you've got to say?'

'What else am I to say?' But her bitterness drove composure away again and she crossed her arms over her stomach, rocking slightly, her dark head bent. 'Oh, God! Am I never to be free of it?' she asked in a low agonized voice.

'You have to free yourself, Valentine,' Kemp said sharply. 'Because I doubt if anyone else can do it for you.'

She shook her head, fighting to regain her self-control. The silence between them grew prolonged. Finally she looked up, to find Kemp watching her intently.

'Are you enjoying the spectacle?' she asked with a smile that was both brave and brittle.

'For pity's sake, Valentine!' Kemp exclaimed furiously. He went on more quietly, 'Why do you never cry?'

'You feel I should cry over an act of childish spite?' she countered scathingly.

'Since it appears to have upset you so badly, why not?' he retorted, but not ungently. 'It would be the natural thing to do.'

'Natural, meaning feminine?' Valentine challenged.

'As I've said before, you're incomplete as a woman,' he reminded her expressionlessly.

'Why is it that men always visualize a whole, complete woman as a vulnerable one?' Valentine wondered whimsically. Her face hardened. 'You'll just have to accept that I'm incomplete.'

'I was talking about your refusal ever to give way to tears, not about an absense of vulnerability.'

Valentine regarded him warily. 'Aren't they one and the same thing?'

'How can they be?' he demanded impatiently. 'You never cry, Valentine, but you're one of the most vulnerable women I've ever known. Strong, yet vulnerable at the same time. Only a truly awesome capacity for pain could demand that constant, incredible act, and that determination never to cry.'

Valentine stared at him for a moment longer. Then her head drooped and she smoothed the skirt of her dress with shaking hands.

'You know me,' she acknowledged flatly, helplessly. 'How can you know me so well?'

She was a picture of utter heartbreak, so alone, and so despairing. Kemp stood up, crossing swiftly to her, and pulled her up into his arms.

'Let me help you, Valli,' he urged in a tone she had never heard from him before. 'Forget about the tears, but let me make you whole and well . . . Let me heal you, let me make love to you tonight, darling.'

A sigh came from her and she seemed to collapse against him, letting him take her full weight. It was as if she had come to the end of something, a long struggle or a weary road, and was about to be revived. His arms were strong and supportive about her, binding her to him, and in him was all the strength she would ever need.

'And will you keep me safe?' she asked yearningly. 'Oh, Kemp, I feel as if I've been alone for so long because no one . . . knew me, but you do. So hold me and share your strength with me, if nothing else.'

'I'll keep you safe, my darling. There's no need for you to stand alone,' he reassured her, his lips moving slowly along the line of her cheek, finally finding the sweetness of her mouth.

They drew apart a little and his hands moved to the sides of her face, smoothing back her dark curls and then sliding down to the sides of her neck, his fingers lightly caressing. Valentine's lips moved silently as she tried to form words to express herself. He had never touched her with such tenderness before and the emotion that gripped her was something so profound, so consuming, that she felt as if he had drawn the soul from her.

'Valentine!' A light flared in Kemp's eyes and they kissed again, a long kiss of hungry passion, and Valentine felt his rising hardness even as her own throbbing desire became paramount need.

'I want you,' he said urgently. 'My beautiful woman ... I've waited so long, and I can't any longer. I must have you ... Come to bed, Valentine.'

There was a wonderful clarity in her eyes as she looked back at him, and a purity of beauty such as her face had never contained before.

'Yes,' she said simply. 'Kemp ... Ah, God, yes! Only you can make me whole.'

There was no hesitation at the door to Valentine's own bedroom. They passed on to Kemp's with its wide luxurious bed. Just for a fleeting moment, as he was swiftly turning down the coverings, there was panic and she glanced anxiously at the dressing-table, but no photograph stood there now. The room was Kemp's now, bearing the imprint of his personality.

Then they were in each other's arms again, helping each other to undress and collapsing on to the bed together, and the long weeks of hunger they had both endured gave an unrestrained tempestuousness to their embrace.

'I want you to know,' she whispered. 'I recognized you, knew you, the first time I looked at you.'

Lamps burned at either side of the bed and Kemp didn't switch them off. 'I want to experience you with every sense . . . I want to see you. You're so beautiful, so incredibly beautiful, Valentine . . . God, but I want you!'

His fingers were gentle on her, finding proof of her arousal, and then his mouth was warmly caressing on her erect nipples.

'I love you, Kemp.' In a shivery voice, she gave him the last truth.

He lifted his head to look into her eyes and the line of his mouth became miraculously tender. 'I know you do, Valli,' he said reassuringly, and put his mouth to hers again while beneath him her flawless body moved in undulating invitation, craving the so long denied consummation of their mutual passion.

'Kemp!'

Their bodies moved, illuminated by the soft light, each arousing the other to greater heights of desire. Guided by instinct, Valentine let her hands and lips touch him in ways that caused him to catch his breath, stroking him, loving him, wanting only to please.

'I'll never let you go,' he told her unsteadily, and groaned as she offered him her lips once more.

'I don't want you to. I'll only ever be safe with you,' she declared passionately. 'Oh, Kemp, I love you . . . I love you so much!'

She felt his thighs between her legs and an awesome trembling started as she lay waiting for him, ready . . .

'You're so perfect,' he said hoarsely, his breathing rapid and shallow, and she saw the blazing pride and desire in the blue eyes and cried out. The tanned skin was stretched tautly across his face and the last flicker of fear that he might mean to reject her again died in that instant.

She rose to meet him, gasping as he entered her, welcoming his penetrant, rigid maleness, moulding him within her, and she felt she must surely die of this exquisite pleasure. In the soft light of the lamps, their first coming together ascended, up and up, to a rapture that was almost intolerable. Valentine moaned in a voice she didn't recognize, clinging passionately to him, loving the strong shaft that moved ceaselessly within her, every powerful thrust taking her nearer to complete and utter ecstasy. She cried out when the first deep inner shudder of her woman's experience started. She was possessed, enraptured, and this was her man, contained in her, her man for ever, for all time. Kemp alone controlled her, gave her life. Choked cries of love came from her as the climax of their rapture approached, and then she was sobbing aloud as the final spasm of total ecstasy made her shudder convulsively in his arms.

It was done, and he couldn't leave her. Her face was wet with tears she hadn't been aware of until now, and she couldn't move. A complete relaxation, a deep stillness and a wondrous fulfilment were the aftermath of their passionate joining. She wanted to stay like this for ever, with this deep peace pervading her entire being, slowing the blood in her veins and making her lethargic and utterly content.

It was a long time before Kemp could stir and then he raised himself to look down into her face.

'Are you all right?' he asked her with a tenderness she could hardly credit.

Valentine's lips curved into a slow beautiful smile and her eyes glowed with the memory of a rich rapture. 'More than,' she said on a sigh. 'Oh, God, Kemp! What did you do to me?'

'I made you complete, Valentine,' he said on a note of unbelievable gentleness. 'You're whole now, aren't you?'

'Yes,' she breathed, the joy and wonderment still suffusing her face. She shivered. 'I never knew ... I never knew what it would be, how it would be ...'

His lips caressed the dampness of her cheeks, moving slowly against them. 'Whole and healed and well ... and all mine, my darling?'

'I feel I've belonged to you for ever, from before the beginning of time,' she said with languorous, luxurious kisses of her own for the beloved face.

He raised his head a little and drew a quiet breath at

the sight of her exquisite face, the lips generous and tender, the eyes deep wells of fulfilment. 'God, Valentine, you're more beautiful now than you've ever been before. Did I really do that to you?'

'Don't you know?' she asked in a shivery voice, and her smile was like a gradual dawn, slow and infinitely lovely.

'And don't you know what you did to me, my beautiful, unbelievable woman who must have been created by angels?' He smiled into her eyes and his arms tightened about her. 'God, Valentine, I never knew anything like the quality of your loving. You give so much.'

She shifted until she had a hand free to explore his face, the fingertips moving delicately and wonderingly over his high cheekbones, and she smiled when his lips moved against her hand. They had loved and now they looked, their faces close, their murmurings finally dying. Then Kemp lifted himself to pull up the covers before one long arm reached for the switch that could control both lamps. It was then that she saw the scratches she had inflicted on his brown shoulders.

'I'm sorry,' she said as the room was plunged into darkness, her hands finding his shoulders, her fingers lightly caressing. 'I didn't know . . . I didn't realise.'

'They're a compliment, Valli,' he said, and she heard the smile in his voice as he gathered her close. 'They honour me . . . I'm glad you never had any other lovers. That too is an honour.'

Later, when she thought he slept, more tears came, of a different nature this time. At first, lightheaded, she had been content to simply lie there in the shelter of his strong arms, revelling in the feeling that she had at last come to a place where she would be safe for evermore.

But the mind was a cruel master. She had known what she was doing earlier, accepting the need to sacrifice part of a dream in return for the fulfilment only Kemp could give her, but it was only now that she realised the full extent of the compromise she had made. She had settled for less than the whole she had wanted, because Kemp would never love her and therefore never marry her. It was less with regret than with sadness and resignation that she wept now. His desire would have to be enough and it was better than nothing, even if it was subtly blended with the wish to achieve revenge through her humiliation.

Because, to Valentine, the position of being his mistress was a humiliating one. Yet she would accept it because he gave her safety, understanding and physical fulfilment. She thought he probably found her desirable enough to keep her as his mistress for years, possibly even after he married, and she was so utterly his that she would be unable to protest. He owned her, heart, body and soul.

She tried to stifle the sobs that tore at her, afraid of waking him. She remembered the threats he had made on Valentine's Day and realised how well he had succeeded in carrying them out, and how subtly, because in bringing her to her knees, all pride vanquished, humbly ready to accept only that part of himself which he would give her and not ask for more, he had still given her so very much. He had brought her to full vital life, making her complete as a woman, and she would know again and again that insurmountable ecstasy and its subsequent peace, the sensation of having found a haven. He had promised that she would not be alone again and that he would keep her safe, and in a strange way, the keeping of those promises would be his revenge.

Dear God, he had even made her cry.

She tried to move away from him as grief racked her body, but the arm lying across her suddenly tightened and she realised he was awake.

'Valentine!'

'Well, you wanted me to cry,' she reminded him sadly.

'But not like this.' He drew her close. 'Never like this. Valentine, let this be an end of such terrible suffering. We're at a beginning now, my darling, something new and wonderful that isn't going to leave time or room for sorrow . . .'

'Let me cry now and I won't again,' she sobbed against the warm curve of his neck. 'I know you'll keep me safe, Kemp.'

'Yes.'

He pacified her with murmured words and soothing caresses, till the tears ceased and his strong stroking hands had stilled the trembling of the slender body. Then he aroused her again, delicately and skilfully, waiting with a fine control until she cried out for him to take her.

'I could die in you like this,' Kemp groaned and, in the last convulsion of ultimate, unparalleled ecstasy, Valentine knew finally and for ever that this joining with the man she loved mattered far, far more than anything else in the world.

She slipped down into a deep, dreamless sleep then, with Kemp's head a sweet weight against her breasts, and when she awoke early in the morning, no doubts came to torment her again. She looked at his face, now beside hers on the pillows, felt the warmth of the relaxed hand lying against the curve of her waist, and knew that she could regret nothing. She was as sure now as she had been in that first uncanny moment of recognition that Kemp was her destiny.

He awoke a little later to find her watching him in the pearly light of a new day, but the light making her eyes lustrous came from within. The serenity of fulfilment seemed to bathe the flawless surfaces and hollows of her face, and he smiled lazily on seeing the vibrant gloriousness he had created in her.

'Well, my Valli?' he questioned her gently. 'No more tears? Have the shadows gone?'

'No more tears, Kemp.'

She raised herself on one elbow to lean over him, searching his face. She smiled tenderly at what she saw. Her fingers and lips touched his face and his bright almost-fair hair, and a new pride came to replace that which he had taken from her: the pride of womanhood, because she realised that he was more content and relaxed than she had ever previously seen him. If their relationship fell short of her old ideal, at least she had given to him as he had to her. The fine lines about his eyes seemed to have been smoothed, and his lips were without the familiar ironic twist. She drew a quick breath of pride and pleasure as she recalled his shattering reaction to her in the night, and finally understood what she could do to and for him.

'I'll be everything you need me to be, Kemp,' she promised in an excess of adoration and gratitude. 'Everything you want me to be.'

'My generous Valentine.' She felt his lips smile as she touched them with her own. 'You're everything I want already . . . perfect as you are.'

'You're all that matters. I love you so much.' Her voice quivered with emotion.

His arms came round her as he buried his face in the warm silken tangle of curls, his mouth against the smoothness of her neck.

'God, Valentine!' His voice was oddly shaken as he turned her on to her back. 'You inspire endless desire. I've ached for you through all the days and nights, and having possessed you at last I know I'll never stop wanting you.'

'Kemp . . . my darling!' Valentine's voice cracked with emotion and she began to shake, arching towards him as she felt his hands on her softly swelling breasts.

Valentine didn't count the days. Still less did she count the nights. It was the hours that she counted; those hours when they had to be apart, she dealing with the visiting public while Kemp was busy with the estate's office work or inspecting the vineyards. Occasionally she would see him when she conducted visitors on a tour of the production cellar and their eyes would meet, full of smiling promise, and once he came to her when she sent Maude for help because a visitor had made Fleurmont the last stop at the end of a day of sampling every wine on every estate and co-operative on the route and his distressed wife couldn't persuade him to get into the car.

'Does that happen often?' Kemp asked grimly when they had gone, with the wife driving.

'Hardly at all, I imagine,' she assured him. 'It's the first time in my experience.'

'I don't like your being exposed to the sort of suggestion he was making.'

'I'm glad you were near enough to come,' she said, moved by his words and by the protective strength of the hand clasping hers as they walked towards the house.

Later she worked out that it had lasted for five days, but at the time she was unaware of past or future. Only the present was of any moment and it was a present filled with tenderness, passion, harmony and laughter. If this was Kemp's revenge, he had the finesse never to remind her of it. Occasionally he talked to her of his longing to return to his chosen career, but it was clear that he had made no decision yet and Valentine was able to avoid wondering what plans he would make for her if he decided to go away.

It was a time during which Valentine felt as if she blossomed into new life. She was more complete than she had ever been before. Kemp also told her that she had grown more beautiful and the mirror confirmed this.

Kemp watched her do her make-up in the mornings with amused interest.

'A work of art,' he commented once, coming to stand behind her as she sat at the dressing-table. 'Beauty concealing beauty.'

Valentine leaned back against him. 'You feel it's unnecessary?'

'No, I like it,' he told her. 'I'd rather the world never saw the Valli I know. I don't want to share her. Flushed and vulnerable, her lips quivering and her voice tremulous with emotion . . . That one is mine.'

'Yes,' she sighed contentedly, her eyes still aglow with the memory of the intimacies they had shared yet again during the night.

'Incidentally,' he went on, 'do you still mind my calling you Valli?'

'Not the way you say it now, darling,' she assured him, her eyes lifted trustingly to his face in the mirror.

He seemed about to say something, but evidently changed his mind, bending to kiss her cheek instead.

He frequently teased her about her lethargy in the mornings for, after spending the night in his arms, Valentine found it difficult to get out of bed. She had cancelled all her dates with Adam and Gary. One night Kemp took her to a small restaurant in Stellenbosch where dancing with him had been a joy to bring tears to her eyes, but they had left early and returned to Fleurmont to make love tempestuously while she cried aloud her love for him so that she was hoarse afterwards.

It was, too, a time of learning. Valentine was realising the power of being a woman. She had held Kemp's trembling body in her arms and had learned how to make him groan under the weight of his urgent hunger. They couldn't leave each other alone and Valentine's need was never any less than his for her. Their hands and lips learned every inch of each other's bodies until they were able to arouse each other to such a finely wrought pitch of clamorous desire that their every union was a wild, rapturous coming together which left them spent and shaken. Valentine learned about passion and tenderness, and never ceased to be grateful for his allowing his victory over her to take this wonderful form which also gave her fulfilment even as it humbled her, and thus a strange victory of her own, a woman's victory.

Five days then, as Valentine later calculated, or rather, five nights. The fifth morning after their becoming lovers was a Saturday and Sylvie Hattingh had agreed to take over Valentine's duties for that morning. Valentine felt as if she was living close to heaven, but there were prosaic matters demanding her attention. Salome dealt with grocery shopping for the household but Valentine was running out of shampoo and moisturiser and she wanted to go into Stellenbosch to purchase them.

'Since Sylvie is taking over for the whole morning, I think I'll stay in bed for a while and go to Stellenbosch later,' she told Kemp who had just returned to the bedroom after a shower.

'Lazy,' he teased, coming to sit on the edge of the bed. He sobered. 'Am I making too many demands, my darling?'

She smiled slowly, her dark curls spread out on the pillow. 'Just new demands,' she corrected him with demure mischievousness.

Kemp's long sensitive fingers traced the line of one high cheekbone and his eyes caressed her pale flawless face.

'I'm afraid I have to go as I'm meeting James at the cellar,' he said on a sigh. 'I'll tell Salome to bring you breakfast here. What time will you be back from Stellenbosch?

'In time for lunch,' she told him, capturing his hand and pressing her lips against the insides of his fingers. 'Polo this afternoon?'

'Yes. Do you mind?'

'No, but this time . . . Do you remember the first time we went to the club, Kemp? Everyone looked at us and I felt so proud to be with you. I wanted to take your arm . . . This time I will.'

'I'm afraid no one will be very surprised,' he laughed. 'They all seemed to make up their minds fairly early that you and I would end up the way we have.'

'I recognised that you were right for me the first time I saw you,' she reminded him. 'I suppose they did too.'

'Ah, that party,' he said reminiscently. 'I wasn't sure what you were all about. I didn't trust you at all, but I knew one thing—I wanted you. I looked at you and, arrogant as it sounds, decided I was the only man present who was worthy of you.'

'Very arrogant . . . and very clever.' She smiled, lifting her slim arms to encircle his neck. 'No one else could have ... fulfilled me as you have done and are doing. Truly, you did make me whole, Kemp.'

His kiss was incredibly tender, and Valentine was smiling when he left the room because she felt as if the loss of her pride was nullified by her supreme happiness.

CHAPTER TEN

VALENTINE showered and dressed in leisurely fashion after Salome, who knew all about her and Kemp and signified her approval with many smiles, had brought her a light breakfast.

Marriage and a honeymoon would have been nice, she thought for the first time, when she was driving to Stellenbosch later, through the autumn gold of the countryside in April. But the thought wasn't wistful, merely humorous, since she had accepted that marriage was out of the question. It was just that she understood one of the practical purposes of honeymoons. They gave new lovers a chance to adapt, gradually, because the intrusions of normal everyday life were suspended. Becoming Kemp's lover when there was still work to be done every morning was somewhat shattering since she had to submerge the sublime spendour of the night in order to contend with the prosaic demands of the day.

She didn't linger over her shopping. There was one other visit to make before filling up with petrol, and then she drove back to Fleurmont at the maximum permissible speed. She was looking forward to going to the polo club that afternoon. No one they knew had been at the restaurant they had gone to a couple of nights ago, so this would be their first public appearance since becoming lovers. Valentine smiled, feeling a grateful affection for all those who had recognised the elemental attraction which bound her to Kemp. They deserved to know they had been right.

When she arrived back at Fleurmont, she recognised Emma Ducaine's red car with a sigh of regret. She wondered if Kemp would tell the girl about them or leave her to discover the truth for herself. Either way, Emma would be hurt, Valentine thought compassionately, but perhaps the wound would heal swiftly because the Kemp she loved was not the real Kemp, but an ideal figure she had built up in her imagination.

They were at the garden table and she went towards them, hoping there would be no unpleasant confrontation with Emma. Hope surged as she saw the third figure because surely Emma would contain her hostility in the presence of an uninvolved witness.

Valentine went on towards them, a tall slender figure in a soft clinging dress with small red and blue geometric shapes on a cream background. She wondered who the other woman was. She hesitated almost imperceptibly. There had been a small blurred photograph in a newspaper once, but when she had realised who the subject was she had turned the page quickly . . . But then she saw Kemp notice her approach, rise swiftly and come towards her.

The expression on his face confirmed what seconds before she had dismissed as a wild suspicion. His eyes were hard and brilliant, and his mouth was twisted in a way she had not seen for days.

He stopped in front of her so that her face was screened from the two women.

'Rose is here, my darling,' he said quietly, and put his hands to her waist as he saw her sway.

Valentine stiffened, but her eyes were dark with anguish. 'Please, Kemp, don't make me meet her,' she whispered brokenly.

She would never again be as degraded as she was in that moment, reduced to begging.

'You're guilty of nothing, Valentine, so you can face her with courage. She is expecting to meet you,' Kemp added.

'While I come unprepared for the meeting.' She spoke through stiff lips and the wounded look in her eyes was giving way to hatred. Her red mouth tightened. 'All right, Kemp, but it's the last you'll ever have from me.'

She stepped away from him without waiting for a reply and walked swiftly to the table, but his hand was at her back as he introduced her to Rose de Villiers and, strangely, she could still draw strength from his touch. But it was mostly hatred that bore her up. Bitterness was like acid in her, making her smiles brittle and her eyes over-bright. She dared not think, not while Rose was still here, lest she give way beneath a welter of pain. She would see this through if it killed her. Her hatred extended to Emma too; why had Kemp involved her in this scene? Simply because he knew Valentine would hate having this final humiliation witnessed by the girl? But she would not give them the satisfaction of seeing her crushed.

Rose de Villiers was a woman of about thirty-five, tall and angular, yet a beauty. Valentine recognised the assistance of henna in the red hair, and the face was an experienced one. At first her attitude towards Valentine was polite but wary, but gradually she relaxed, perhaps seeing the fear and irrational shame that lay beyond the bitter-sweet smiles of the vivid lips and the hardness of the sapphire eyes.

'It's so long since I've been to Fleurmont,' Rose said reflectively after a few minutes during which conversation had been polite and banal. 'Do you enjoy working here, Miss McLaren?'

'I have enjoyed it, yes,' Valentine replied in a tone rich with meaning and Kemp gave her a sharp glance. Looking unconcerned, she took a sip from the glass of semi-sweet rosé he had given her. 'Are you up from Cape Town for the day?'

'I'm actually staying in Stellenbosch for a few days. I've a friend on the university staff.' She paused, looking at her watch. 'In fact, I imagine he'll start wondering where I am if I don't get back soon. You did say you'd drive me back to town, didn't you, Emma?'

'Of course,' Emma agreed reluctantly. 'But it's early yet.'

'Won't you join us for lunch?' Valentine invited charmingly, addressing herself to Rose, and Kemp smiled a little grimly while Emma looked disconsolate.

'Thanks all the same, but no.' Rose's smile was kind. 'I really feel I must get back, but first ... It was Maude who brought the drinks out. Is Salome still with you? I must just say hullo to her. Come and help me find her, Miss McLaren?'

'She ought to be in the kitchen,' said Valentine, standing up and flinging an insouciant smile at Kemp and Emma. The effort made her feel sick.

Out of sight of the others, Rose came to a halt. 'Salome can wait for a few minutes, Valli ... I'm sorry, I noticed Kemp calls you Valentine, but you see, I've always thought of you as Valli. I couldn't say this in front of them since we were all being so sociable, pretending nothing was wrong ... I want you to know that I think this was a vile, cruel thing to do to you.'

'I would agree with that,' Valentine said drily.

'You were totally unprepared, weren't you?' Rose said sympathetically. 'I'm more sorry than I can say, since I can imagine your feelings only too well. I didn't know until I got here that I would be meeting you, or I'd never have come. It was a casual invitation and I felt like seeing Fleurmont again. I didn't want to hurt or embarrass you.'

'No. Others wanted to do that,' Valentine murmured bitterly.

They looked at each other sadly, and each saw that like herself the other had suffered. There was recognition, an exchange of understanding.

'You've suffered terribly over what Philip did, haven't you?' Rose guessed, sighing. 'Since I've unwittingly inflicted my presence on you and probably revived the whole tragic business in your mind, we might as well extract some benefit from the situation. I've often thought of you, wondering what had become of you ... My hus-

band did a terrible thing to you. I would like you to
know that I've never blamed you for what happened. I
knew Philip too well, you see. His infatuation must have
been monumental, but you weren't to know what your
rejection would do, and even if you could have known
. . . No, you had to be true to yourself, and Philip needed
a woman who would be mother as well as lover to him. I
don't think you could have filled that rôle. Oh, my dear,
I can see I'm distressing you.'

'No . . . no!' Valentine assured her, but her hands were
clenched, her nails digging into her palms. 'It has . . . It
does help me to hear this. The worst times have always
been when I've thought of you, and the shock and hurt
you must have felt. I could see most of the situation fairly
rationally, but I felt a sense of . . . of shame, guilt or
something, where you were concerned, even though he
hadn't told me about you.'

'Poor Philip,' Rose commented, and Valentine had the
impression it was something she had said many times
before. 'But you must put away such feelings now, Valli.
I've met a man, one who, though he occasionally leans on
me, also allows me to lean, instead of expecting me to do
all the encouraging and supporting. That's the way it
should be. I've been . . . healed, so you must be too.'

'I thought I had been,' Valentine said, more to herself
than to the other woman. How stupid she had been!

'You're young . . . But I can see you're still upset,' Rose
digressed. 'Come, I'll just say hullo to Salome, and then
Emma can take me back to town and you can forget this
unfortunate encounter.'

If only it was so simple!

Not many minutes passed before Rose was saying
goodbye to Kemp. Emma was already in her car with the
engine running, a distinctly sulky expression on her face,
while Kemp was at his most inscrutable, but Valentine
couldn't bring herself to wonder what had passed between
them while she and Rose had been absent.

'Keep in touch, Rose,' Kemp was saying.

'I will.' Rose gave Valentine a smiling glance. 'Perhaps after a time we'll all be able to get together one evening.'

Valentine smiled automatically, wondering if she really believed that. If she did, Rose was crediting her with less pride and more resilience than she possessed.

The red car pulled away and Valentine looked at Kemp sadly. For the moment his attention was on Rufus. The dog had been rolling somewhere and his beautiful red coat had little sticks and leaves in it which Kemp was removing.

Wordlessly, Valentine turned and went towards the house.

'Valentine.'

She was at the front door when she heard him, but she neither paused nor looked back.

He found her in the main bedroom, sweeping the pots and tubes of make-up she had used that morning into the large box which normally contained them.

'Are you all right?' He stopped, realising what she was doing, and his eyes narrowed. 'What are you doing?'

Valentine straightened and looked at him with eyes that burned.

'Preparing to leave,' she said succinctly.

'May I ask why?' he enquired levelly.

'Do you have to?' she retorted with a graceful lift of one shoulder. Her control snapped. 'My God! You realised that morning you told me Rose was seeing someone from Stellenbosch . . . You realised then what it would do to me to be brought face to face with her, so you deliberately went ahead and arranged it. I've been so . . . so stupid! I really thought your desire for revenge had been satisfied by the fact that you had robbed me of all pride by making me your lover without loving me . . . listening to me tell you a thousand times how much I loved you, knowing I practically worshipped you . . . And all the time you were planning this, the . . . the ultimate revenge, forcing me to meet the woman . . . Oh, God!'

Kemp's face was a tight mask of anger, the skin stretched tautly across the bones. His eyes blazed and his lips were twisted sardonically.

'This, then, is what you believe of me,' he said distastefully. 'Such faith, sweetheart. Such trust!'

'I did have faith,' she told him in a cold, clear little voice. 'I did trust that having . . . had me, you were done with punishing me. I gave you everything of myself, unreservedly, and I thought you would be content with that; that the fact that you'd humiliated me utterly by taking my . . . my love, would be sufficient, especially as it was a method of revenge from which you too derived personal pleasure. But you had to break me utterly, didn't you? I suppose I was too happy . . . I had reconciled myself to my bondage too easily and wasn't suffering enough to satisfy you.'

'Bondage? To what bondage are you referring?' he enquired silkily.

Valentine closed the make-up box with a loud click and gave him a smile that was tragic in its bitterness.

'Isn't it bondage when a woman is so enslaved by a man that she'll gratefully become his mistress, knowing that his absence of love or respect precludes marriage, and count her pride well lost for the half loaf she's granted? Isn't that bondage, Kemp?' she accused tartly. 'Except that in our case there wasn't merely an absence of love and respect on your part, but active contempt as well.'

'You insult both yourself and me with such talk,' Kemp said furiously. 'If that's what . . . Go then, Valentine. I want nothing more of you.'

'I'm going,' she confirmed icily. 'Today. Sylvie will have to do my job until you employ a replacement. Tell her I'm sorry.'

'Is that all you're sorry about?' he taunted. 'My God! You've professed a great deal of love over the last few days, but it's a small and tawdry love, not to mention immature, that can react this way.'

'You believe it should be so great a love that I'd stay

with you no matter what you did to me?' Valentine enquired sweetly. 'But you see, Kemp, some pride was left to me after all. I do love you—I should hate you now, but I don't. I love you and I'm not ashamed of it. Nor should you be—my love is something worth having, but not even you may treat me as you have today. I won't tolerate it.'

'Yes, I too thought your love was something worth having,' he flung at her. 'It proves worthless, though, when it . . . Just go, Valentine.'

She snatched up what belongings she had already put together, adding the make-up box to the top of the pile, and walked out of the room with her head held high, going to her old bedroom to pack since much of her property had remained there.

Anger and resentment sustained her as she filled her suitcases. She had no thoughts, only feelings, and those feelings were extreme. Pride was a violent thing, obliterating everything else, and that pride was incensed by what Kemp had done in his final attempt to humiliate her. She did not have to endure such contempt, not from anyone. She was worthy of more consideration, especially from one to whom she had given her love.

She took the time to renew her make-up before taking the cases out to her car. Only when they were safely stowed in the boot and she herself was sitting in the driver's seat, fastening her safety belt, did Kemp reappear.

'Where will you be going?' he asked coldly through the open window.

Valentine lifted a shoulder. 'Home, I suppose. Gordon's Bay. I have nowhere else to go at the moment.'

He seemed to think for a moment. 'You need not fear that I shall come after you——'

'Your desire for revenge is finally sated then?' she enquired sardonically, arching an eyebrow.

'God damn you, Valentine,' he said very quietly.

'I'm beginning to believe I was damned at birth,' she retorted bitterly.

He drew a deep breath. 'If our relationship, our very brief relationship,' he amended ironically, 'should have consequences for you, will you let me know?'

'If I should be pregnant? I'm almost sure I'm not.' Her laughter was a mockery, too close to tears. 'It's funny, isn't it? After I'd done my shopping in Stellenbosch this morning, I went to a doctor and got a prescription for something to prevent pregnancy ... They won't be needed now, will they?'

He shook his head. 'You bitch! Go!'

Valentine turned the key and he stepped away from the car. She looked at him, saw the harsh grooves bracketing his twisted mouth and the way the lines seemed to be cut into the tanned skin about his eyes. Anguish tore at her, a physical pain, and she spoke to him once more.

'Why do I have to love you so much?' she asked despairingly. 'Why did you do it, Kemp? How could you? I hope you suffer as much as I will. You can search the world and you won't find a woman who can give you as much as I can, because you'll never find a woman who loves you as much as I do!'

Then, biting hard on her lower lip, she put the car into gear with a jerk, released the brake and drove away. She had her last sight of him in her rear-view mirror, standing there in his casual clothes with the autumn sun brightening his hair.

'Oh, God ... Kemp!' she whispered agonisedly.

Away from Fleurmont she had to pull over to the side of the main road. She crossed her arms over the steering-wheel and rested her head on them, but the tears she had anticipated didn't come. Strangely, all at once, she felt nothing. She was cold and empty, dead inside, and she didn't think she would ever feel again.

After a while, her white face set in a hard, composed mask, she started the car again and began the long drive to Gordon's Bay.

*

'Val, love, you cannot continue like this,' Nigel said emphatically.

'What do you suggest I do, then?' she challenged bitterly.

'I don't know,' Nigel sighed. 'Something, anything, just to end this terrible suffering. Go back to this man, or write to him ... Let me go and see him and find out if perhaps your mind hasn't exaggerated what he did to you. You were clearly expecting persecution, taking his wish for revenge for granted, and perhaps you overreacted.'

'No, Nigel.' Valentine's arm, linked with his, trembled. 'One of the things he said to me that last day was ... that he wanted nothing more of me.'

'I wish I could help.'

It was two weeks and a day since Valentine had left Fleurmont. At first, the deadness of feeling had remained with her, and the absence of all emotion had enabled her to pretend she was not too badly wounded by what had occurred, but then feeling had returned and, with it, unceasing, agonising pain. She yearned for Kemp with a terrible aching hunger which allowed her no rest, and her nights were a hell of tormented longing. She thought that if this anguish continued much longer, she might lose her mind.

Her parents didn't invite her confidence and she didn't give it to them. There had been a gulf between them in her adult years and, while they had accepted her assurances that she had not deliberately hurt Philip de Villiers, they had not truly understood and had been resentful of the publicity engendered by the tragedy. They were two ordinarily good-looking, ordinarily gifted and intelligent people who had produced two exceptional children and now found themselves perplexed more than anything else by their brilliant son and beautiful daughter.

It was Easter Sunday. Nigel had come home for the long weekend and it was to him that Valentine told her story although she gained little relief from doing so. Now, in the late evening, with the light fading from behind the lowering pewter clouds and a fine, cold mist drifting over the bay, brother and sister strolled up and down the beach, arm-in-arm, as they had done all their lives. The last dog walkers had gone, driven home by the chill air, and they were the only figures peopling the bleak scene.

Valentine tried to smile. 'Do you remember when we were children, Nigel, and we used to come and promenade up and down the beach whenever there was a crowd because we were pretty children and we liked the sensation of being stared at? It would be nice to be like that again. Enjoyment was all we knew.'

'No, Val,' Nigel said calmly. 'It wouldn't be nice at all, to remain untouched all our lives. Experience shapes and enriches us. I don't even believe you wholly regret your affair with this Kemp Irvine.'

'You're right,' Valentine conceded flatly. 'I don't regret it. For that short time he made me whole and complete because he's the other half of me . . . But now I'm hollow and empty and, oh God, how am I going to do without him for the rest of my life, Nigel?'

Nigel looked at her compassionately, seeing a study in black and white. Her jeans tucked into boots, her suede jacket over a cashmere sweater; all were black and her face was white and strained. The damp air had curled her hair into dark tendrils about her face, and her eyes were huge and so dark with pain that they too looked black.

'We're very alike, you and I, but I pray God I don't have your truly terrible capacity for suffering,' he said soberly. 'Life has used you badly, hasn't it?'

'But it goes on and on,' said Valentine, thinking of Philip's way out and shuddering.

Perhaps Nigel had the same thought because he said urgently, 'You do know that you'll survive even this, love? 'This too shall pass'. Remember that.'

'Oh, I can go on enduring for ever, Nigel,' she assured him with an intensity of bitterness causing her voice to

shake. 'But it won't pass. Kemp is in me for ever and ever
. . . He's part of me!'

He put his arms round her and let her sob, but tears
brought her no relief and they both knew it.

'Come on, Valentine,' he said when she was quiet
again. 'It's cold and the light is getting worse. Let's go
back to the house.'

'No, you go. I want to walk . . . I've got to walk!'
Valentine said desperately. 'This . . . this thing won't let
me rest. I can't seem to keep still. Trying to relax only
makes me feel worse. I want to be alone now.'

'All right, Garbo, but if you're not home in, say, half
an hour, I'll come and fetch you,' Nigel conceded reluctantly. He put his hands on her shoulders and looked at
her intently. 'Promise me you'll . . . be all right.'

'I promise.' She smiled faintly. 'You know me, Nigel.'

'Of course. I'm sorry.' He grinned engagingly and
turned away, striding over the sand, tall and long-legged,
next to Kemp the most beautiful man Valentine knew.
He waved to her from the empty car park and was swallowed up by the greyness of the evening.

He was lucky, she thought wistfully. His great beauty
had never brought the tragedy that hers had done, perhaps because he was cleverer and therefore warier than
she had been.

Still Valentine paced the deserted beach, her fretful
thoughts wasted because they had all been thought before
and brought no solution. The wind which prevented the
light mist from gathering and becoming thick made her
face icy cold and her fingers felt numb even when she
pushed them into the pockets of her jacket. She was a fool
to stay out here, but her restlessness became torture in the
house perched high above one of the town's winding
roads. She would have to think about a job soon, she
supposed wearily, turning again and walking in the other
direction.

The little waves were torn to rough lace by the wind
and she listened to their lapping sound without pleasure

and wondered what Kemp was doing now. When it got dark she would go home, she decided, otherwise poor Nigel would have to come out in the cold again. Perhaps tonight she would sleep. It was the nights she had learned to dread most, when her longing for Kemp's vibrant possession became unbearable and she would weep bereftly into the pillow, remembering the strength of his arms about her and the reassuring warmth of his body against hers. He had promised to keep her safe . . .

Valentine removed a hand from her pocket and touched her icy cheeks experimentally. They felt damp, whether solely from the mist she wasn't sure. Her make-up, she thought, must have vanished long ago.

The light was fading and the car that turned into the carpark had its headlights on. Valentine was momentarily caught in their powerful beam and she moved hastily into the greyness of the evening. She couldn't see what sort of car it was, but she didn't think Nigel would have come for her just yet, and it wasn't a night for fishing, so the occupants were probably a pair of lovers, she decided with unreasonable resentment as she imagined their happiness, cocooned in the warm darkness of the car.

She walked on steadily, heard a door slam and realised it must be Nigel after all. She turned, full of compunction at having brought him out again, and froze——

'No!' It was a low moan of protest as she recognised the familiar stride of the beloved figure.

Still he came towards her and now Valentine backed away until she had the sea directly behind her.

'Go away!' She raised her voice. 'Oh, God, haven't you had enough from me without this too . . . Go away, Kemp!'

'Valentine!' His voice was urgent.

'Go away,' she repeated sharply. 'You can't . . . I won't let you see me like this. I haven't . . . got my act together yet. Have a little mercy on me, Kemp.'

'For pity's sake, Valentine——'

'Pity! What do you know of pity?' she flung at him

bitterly and, as he put out a hand, 'Don't touch me!'

Kemp thrust his hands violently into the pockets of his jacket. 'All right, I won't touch you,' he said wearily. 'But will you listen to me, please?'

Valentine stared at him with a mixture of fear and longing, hardly able to credit his presence. He looked tired and his mouth was twisted as if he was in pain.

'What is it?' she asked in a voice as cold and soft as the mist.

For a few moments, he stared at her in silence, noting the pallor and shadows suffering had wrought, and the brittle tension of her. She looked as fragile as crystal, as if a touch might shatter her, and the control she had over herself now was heartrendingly frail.

'Valentine, will you please tell me how I came to fail you so badly?' he requested jerkily. 'How I failed you to the extent that you could imagine our lovemaking was an act of revenge on my part, and then believe that I would deliberately invite Rose to Fleurmont?'

'Well, didn't you?' she flung at him tartly.

'No, damn you, I did not!' he exclaimed savagely. 'That was Emma's doing as I'd have expected you to realise. She met Rose in Stellenbosch and persuaded her that she ought to visit Fleurmont, never mentioning your presence. I was appalled when they arrived, appalled for your sake . . . Name of God, Valli, how could you think I'd want to do that to you?'

'But didn't you do it to me?' she lashed out of the depths of her unhappiness.

He looked at the dark tragic eyes, and the quivering lips she was pathetically trying to control, and he swore. 'You don't believe me, do you?'

'How can I?'

'Doesn't it stand to reason?' he demanded impatiently. 'Emma it was who sent those press-cuttings, Emma it was who left that message on your mirror . . . Valentine, she'd probably admit it if you challenged her with it. And Rose would tell you how her presence on Fleurmont came about.'

'If it's true, then why didn't you tell me at the time?' she asked sceptically, realising that her teeth were chattering.

He sighed heavily. 'Because I was so damned furious at your lack of trust in me, the small faith ... That you could believe such a thing of me. I stayed angry for days, Valentine, but eventually I started wondering if it wasn't due to some lack in myself that you'd believed what you did. What did I do, or fail to do, that you could believe I'd taken you in revenge for Philip?'

Valentine had begun to weep, bitterly, and the tears were warm as they trickled down her cold face. 'You said that was what you would do ... the day you learned who I really was. Valentine's Day,' she gulped.

'I was furious that day as well, because you hadn't told me yourself,' Kemp said curtly. 'I stayed angry for precisely that one day, Valli ... and part of that night, as you know. I know I was often angry after that, but that was because you were so slow in learning to trust me ... I wanted you to realise for yourself that I didn't blame you for what Philip had done. You used to punish yourself ... I would get impatient, waiting for you, but I had to let you learn for yourself, and learn to trust me, after the way I'd behaved that night ... And then there was another delay when you resented me because I wouldn't make love to you in that field of flowers, but you still didn't trust me that day. Then you had that idea of seducing me, and I didn't want it to be that way, although God knows how I prevented myself from taking what you were offering. When we did finally become lovers, I thought all your doubts had gone ... And now I know that all the time you were imagining yourself in a bondage situation. Dear God, how could you fail to realise that everything you felt, I felt with equal intensity?'

'You couldn't,' she protested weakly.

'Couldn't what?'

'Feel as I did. I loved you. I still love you.'

'As I love you,' he said simply, but then—'Valentine, my darling, what have I done?'

Because she had fallen to her knees, still weeping, and he bent and lifted her to her feet, holding her against him, his arms strong about her, and she realised that he was rigid with tension.

'You never told me you loved me,' she said brokenly.

'Valli, don't—don't cry like this. I can't bear it, seeing my beautiful, strong, brave, clever woman so ... so crushed. Oh, don't, darling!' One hand came up to the back of her head, pressing her against him, and she buried her face against his suede-covered shoulder. 'People say "I love you" every day and it can mean everything or nothing. I thought I was showing you I loved you in a hundred ways ... I feel now that I failed you. I should have known Philip's death still haunted you. So often I wanted to reassure myself, but then I'd look at your lovely radiant face and be afraid of seeing a shadow there, if I mentioned his name. If only I'd risked it, I could have convinced you and none of this ... this pain would have been necessary.'

'It was all ... done in love, then?' she asked against his shoulder, hardly daring to believe it.

'So much love. Couldn't you tell?' he asked reproachfully, then sighed. 'No, of course you couldn't. The idea that I was punishing you for Philip was too deeply rooted, wasn't it? Can you believe in me now, Valentine? Now that I've told you in words ... Come back to me, my darling. These last two weeks I've been in hell ... I love you beyond belief. I'd take the world and break it and re-make it for you ... Come back to me, Valentine.'

'Yes,' she said simply, and the grief went out of her on a great shuddering sigh as she rested against him.

In the fading light his fingers moved in her dark curls, tipping back her head until he could see her face. His expression softened as he saw the faint anxiety there.

'You will be happy, Valentine,' he promised. 'I know

... I know that you've suffered far more than I'm worth and you can't slide into joy immediately.'

She nodded slightly, no longer surprised by his understanding. 'I feel I wronged you, Kemp, by failing to evaluate your love correctly ... I'm sorry.'

'Ah, don't, darling,' he said urgently, his arms tightening about her again. 'There were things you didn't realise and things I didn't realise, and they've caused us both a lot of pain. I'll tell you I love you every day for the rest of our lives ... And how I love you. You're my woman and I've loved you for ever.'

'Not really,' she corrected with a faint smile, beginning to feel at last. 'You didn't trust me at all to begin with.'

'But I recognised you as my life's mate,' he assured her. 'From the moment I saw you at that party ... For a few days I resisted, but by the morning of Valentine's Day I had capitulated. It seemed so simple. Then that envelope of cuttings arrived and I treated you so brutally that night. When my anger had abated, I realised you were far more complex than I had thought, with great gaping holes in the fabric of your personality, thanks to my cousin, and I knew they'd have to be closed before I could make you mine. When we finally became lovers I thought it would complete the healing process, instead of which ...'

'I was very happy, despite believing what I did,' she told him gently when he broke off with a sigh. 'You weren't to know. I see that now.'

'You said things that day you left ... Valentine, you were not humiliated, or dishonoured. We were lovers first because our need to be was immediate and urgent, but you would have been my wife by now. And you will be, won't you?'

'Soon?' The old, beautiful smile had appeared.

'Very soon, my darling. Just as soon as possible,' he promised her. He smiled too. 'Why are we standing out here on this cold and windy beach in the near dark? Come to the car, Valli.'

'Aren't you going to kiss me?' she asked limpidly.

'Do you want me to?'

'You . . .' She laughed helplessly, coming to full life at last. 'What do you think?'

'All my life to you, Valentine,' he said just before their lips met, and the tender passion of their kiss was equally a pledge.

'Go on talking to me,' she sighed as they walked towards the car, their arms about each other. 'I love the sound of your voice. Tell me how you knew where I was.'

'Ah!' Kemp laughed gently. 'I went out of my mind when I found your parents' house and they didn't know where you were. Then a young man who looks like you arrived, took one look at me and said, "Ah, I knew it was all a ghastly mistake. You've come for Valentine, right?" So I told them I was going to marry you and he said, "Get down to the beach and tell her that." When I left, your mother was planning our wedding and your brother was suggesting that, knowing Valentine, he didn't think you'd agree to white or even cream. What have you told that young man about us?'

Valentine collapsed against him, laughing delightedly. 'He's the only one I've told. Nigel is my dear brother and next to you, he's the person who understands me best . . . And he was right. I won't be married in white, but don't think you've robbed me of that, my darling. I planned my wedding as a little girl and even then I decided against white. I wanted to be different,' she concluded proudly.

'You're an original,' Kemp said with equal pride. 'Incomparable Valentine.'

And she was.

Kemp watched Valentine as she approached on her father's arm a little over a week later. Certain conventions had been adhered to for her parents' sakes, but in most things Valentine had had her way. The church they had chosen was a small one in Cape Town and their guests were few, chosen because they were liked or loved, not for any other reason. Two of his television colleagues were present, and Nigel was looking amused by the whole occasion as he stood beside Mrs McLaren in the front pew. Also present, smiling or emotional depending on their temperaments, were James and Sylvie Hattingh, Freddie and Salome Jansen and Maude who had all driven down from Fleurmont, and behind the bride came her two tiny doll-like attendants, Binnie Hattingh and Trevor Jansen, slightly out of step.

Kemp's eyes met Valentine's sparkling ones and he knew she was giving the performance of her life and revelling in it. She was a wildly romantic figure, the sort of woman most men dream of and never find, in her pale shell-pink confection of a dress with its stiff mid-calf length skirt. Her face was not veiled, and at her throat and ears were tiny gold hearts. Small flowers lay against her glorious dark curls, and she was breathtakingly beautiful, with a beauty which was all Valentine and illuminated from within, since she was wearing less make-up than usual.

Still their eyes remained locked and as soon as she reached his side her hand grasped his and the small secretive smiles they exchanged were in danger of breaking into wide smiles. For a timeless moment they were as if alone. Then the minister coughed warningly——

'You were really enjoying yourself, weren't you?' Kemp teased a short while later in the vestry when they were signing the register.

'Oh, yes!' Her smile was very beautiful. 'I think I'm the happiest, luckiest woman in all the world!'

The minister smiled sympathetically at Kemp. 'You could kiss her properly now,' he suggested, having brought their formal kiss in the church to an end with another of his peculiarly eloquent little coughs.

Valentine seemed to melt into Kemp's arms and the minister turned to talk to Mr and Mrs McLaren, whose relief at the conventional turn taken by their rare, perplexing daughter's life was palpable.

'I've got you for ever now,' said Kemp, having kissed her until she was breathless.

'And I you.' And their eyes and their lips once more promised all that their steady voices had promised during the ceremony.

There were photographs taken in the vestry and then they emerged into the church once more and the radiance of Valentine's face made Salome Jansen weep emotionally while Freddie wore a rare grin.

'Is it wrong of me to feel complacent?' Valentine whispered to Kemp when they posed for more photographs outside, the late afternoon sunshine illuminating their faces.

'I think we've both got a right to feel that way,' Kemp murmured, his eyes blazing with passionate love as he saw the wonderful clarity of hers. 'You look beautiful.'

'So do you.'

Since they were a small party, their reception was held in a hired room at the luxurious hotel where Kemp and Valentine would be spending the night before driving to the cottage on a deserted stretch of coast, lent to them by one of his television friends because they had decided that their honeymoon must be spent far, far from all other members of humanity.

The two television men pretended to be regretful when Valentine left Kemp's side for a moment to speak to them.

'First television lost him, and now the noble brotherhood of bachelors will know him no more,' one said mournfully.

Valentine looked thoughtful. 'I wouldn't be too sure about television having lost him for ever, you know.'

They brightened. 'If you could persuade him to return . . . He's needed, you know, Valentine.'

'I know,' she said proudly. 'But I won't persuade him to do anything. He'll do what's right for him. However, I think I know what that will be.'

She drifted back to Kemp, wondering when she should

broach the subject and deciding that now was not the time. Kemp's arm came round her waist and their eyes met as if they drank of each other. Nigel, who had been talking to Kemp, watched them narrowly and finally gave a relieved smile.

'Oh, you lucky, lucky people,' he said softly, admiring the perfect matching of two people who would draw attention wherever they went. 'You've got a happy ending . . . Safe now, Valentine?'

Valentine leaned against her husband and smiled at each of them in turn. 'Safe for ever, Nigel.'

'I promised you that before, darling,' Kemp reminded her. 'I do so again now with Nigel as witness. I know what a rare and wonderful treasure I have in your sister, and I'll guard her as such.'

Very much later that night in their luxurious hotel suite, Valentine gently disengaged herself from Kemp's arms. With the light still on, he had made love to her with such passion and pride of possession that tears had stung her eyes. In the supreme moment of attaining their personal nirvana she had glimpsed his face and the love blazing there had heightened her ecstasy so that she called his name as a blinding white light of happiness dazzled her mind, before she sank breathlessly back against the pillows, at peace at last.

Now, when her heart's normal rhythm was restored, she stirred.

'Where are you going?'

'I want that champagne we never had,' she told him mischievously, shrugging on a vibrant pink silk robe and going to fetch the ice-bucket in which the bottle reposed. They hadn't needed or wanted it earlier.

He watched indulgently as she opened it, smiling at her laughter when the cork popped and accepting a brimming glass from her hands when she returned to the bed. Valentine plumped up her pillows and reached for her own glass.

'Now—you've to call me Mrs Irvine!'

He raised his glass. 'To you, Mrs Irvine, my wife, the most miraculous woman on this earth . . . God, Valentine, you're beautiful. Are you really mine?'

'We've got papers to prove it now,' she said liltingly, admiring her wedding ring and the sapphire engagement ring he had given her a few days ago. 'I'll never let you go.'

'Really mine,' Kemp repeated reflectively.

For a while she basked in the warmth of his gaze while they sipped their champagne. Her dark hair was a gypsy tangle and her face was radiant, her eyes sparkling and her lips tender from prolonged kisses.

Then she said slowly, 'There's still the matter of our future to discuss.'

'You're my future,' he told her. 'With you beside me, I can bear Fleurmont.'

'You don't have to . . . bear it,' she said carefully, putting down her glass. 'I'm not going to influence you, Kemp, but you must do what you truly want to do.'

'I'd keep Fleurmont either way,' Kemp said thoughtfully. 'But as to where we'll spend most of our time . . . You've loved Fleurmont, haven't you?'

'Yes.' She smiled tenderly, taking his glass away from him and placing it beside hers. 'But I've a greater love than Fleurmont, and one I need more. I want to be with you, Kemp, but I want you fully content in what you're doing and that would seem to mean returning to what is, after all, your chosen life.'

'The places I have to go to are unromantic and lacking in glamour, my darling,' he said gently. 'And you're both romantic and distinctly glamorous . . . How could you endure it?'

'I've had my share of romance, and glamour, and my great moment today . . . Nigel said we had a happy ending, but it's really a happy beginning to our real life together, Kemp,' she said seriously. 'There'd be Fleurmont to come back to occasionally, and more often if we have a child. You're never to feel you're depriving me of anything. All I ask is to be with you. It doesn't matter at this moment, but promise me you'll choose what you truly want most.'

'I promise you, my darling,' he said quietly.

'Thank you.' She knew what his choice would be, but it didn't matter because she had spoken no less than the truth about requiring only to be with him. 'You see, your happiness is mine.'

'Oh, Valentine, my darling!' He reached for the unmatched loveliness that was all his to treasure and pleasure. 'You're so generous and feminine and—whole, a complete woman.'

'Made so by you.' Her robe was slipping from one smooth shoulder, revealing the tender curve of a pale breast as their endless passion flared anew. 'Oh, Kemp ... my husband, but still my lover for all time.'

Love and desire lit his eyes as he leaned over her exquisite beauty, and his mouth was tender.

'You're right,' he murmured. 'This is a happy beginning.'

Harlequin Plus
THE TRADITION OF VALENTINES

No one is really certain just when and where the tradition of exchanging love tokens on Saint Valentine's feast day – February 14 – began, though it probably had its origins in ancient pagan Roman fertility rites held in mid-February.

It was in the late Middle Ages and early Renaissance in England that the occasion gained its greatest popularity. February 14 became the day to get engaged or to give gifts of love – modest or lavish. On that day, too, those who were looking for a lover or spouse could draw lots. In one custom the names of young unmarried women were put into a box, and each man drew his valentine for the year; in another, the first young man a girl saw in the morning became her special suitor for the year.

By the 1660s, at the time of the Restoration, the lot could fall to married as well as single persons, and gifts were de rigueur. Samuel Pepys records in his diary that his wife received from Sir William Batten "half-a-dozen pair of gloves and a pair of silk stockings and garters for her valentine."

Within a hundred years, love tokens or prettily written letters had replaced expensive gifts; in the 1840s, with the advent of cheap postage, the paper valentine became the fashion. In England and America during the Victorian era, valentines were handmade in fanciful and extravagant designs from the finest papers, embellished with such materials as velvet, feathers, pressed ferns, shells, glass beads and perfume.

Today some of the old customs are still carried on. Schoolchildren draw for their valentines. And lovers of all ages exchange cards and gifts—not gloves and garters, but red roses, perfume, jewelry and chocolate.

Yours **FREE**, with a home subscription to **SUPERROMANCE**™

Complete and mail
the coupon below today!

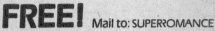

- -

FREE! Mail to: SUPERROMANCE

In the U.S.
2504 West Southern Avenue
Tempe, AZ 85282

In Canada
649 Ontario St.
Stratford, Ontario N5A 6W2

YES, please send me FREE and without any obligation, my
SUPERROMANCE novel, LOVE BEYOND DESIRE. If you do not hear
from me after I have examined my FREE book, please send me the
4 new **SUPERROMANCE** books every month as soon as they come
off the press. I understand that I will be billed only $2.50 for each book
(total $10.00). There are no shipping and handling or any other hidden
charges. There is no minimum number of books that I have to
purchase. In fact, I may cancel this arrangement at any time.
LOVE BEYOND DESIRE is mine to keep as a FREE gift, even if
I do not buy any additional books.

NAME	(Please Print)

ADDRESS	APT. NO.

CITY

STATE/PROV.	ZIP/POSTAL CODE

SIGNATURE (If under 18, parent or guardian must sign.)   **134 BPS KAKG**

SUP-SUB-1

This offer is limited to one order per household and not valid to present
subscribers. Prices subject to change without notice.
Offer expires August 31, 1984

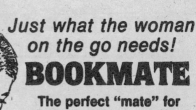